Praise for Siren Promised

"Using Alan M. Clark's gorgeously dark fantastique artwork to springboard the lush, compelling, often raw storyline forward, Johnson and Clark have created a unique literary atmosphere full of dread and wonder. This is a synergistic fusion of major talents that seethes with the black, beautiful energy of nightmares made real."

—Tom Piccirilli
author of *Headstone City* and *A Choir of Ill Children*

"I have just one word for you – DAMN! The authors make you live through it, rather than just read about it. The power of Clark and Johnson working together is in their ability to blur the lines in the tale and touch you where it counts. By the time I was done reading I was wondering about the purpose in my own life; they left me with an emptiness I didn't even know existed."

—Horror-Web.com

"Siren Promised is a page-turner. Johnson and Clark are masters of their crafts and have turned in a gripping, frightening piece of work that shows that real life, the people we know, and we our-selves can be more horrifying than any made-up monster or ghoul."

—Verbicide

"Siren Promised is a tale of addiction and legacy and rebirth. It is spontaneous and compelling. Dark, sordid characters, bound to gether like weaving vines of a bog rose. A haunting tale that will surprise you constantly. I recommend it highly."

— Cemetery Dance Weekly

Siren Promised

Jeremy Robert Johnson & Alan M. Clark

Publishing

Eugene, Oregon
2017

The paperback of Siren Promised was originally published by SwallowDown Press

"Siren Promised" copyright © 2017 Jeremy Robert Johnson & Alan M. Clark

All illustrations in this book copyright © 2017 Alan M. Clark

Introduction "Siren Promised—From Hell" © 2017 Simon Clark

ISBN: 978-0-9965536-9-8

IFD Publishing
P.O. Box 40776
Eugene, OR 97404
U.S.A.

Book design by Alan M. Clark

Printed in the United States of America

Dedication

For those who have fought to become clean and sober.
Keep fighting.

Acknowledgments

Alan is an alcoholic.
Jeremy is a drug addict.
Acknowledgment is the first step.

Jeremy would like to thank:
Bayard—for opening the door.
Alan M. Clark—for the chance.
Jessica Wicklund—for showing the way.
The Johnson Family—for giving me life and making it worth living.

Alan would like to thank:
Joan Clark—for many years of unwavering moral support and much love.
Elizabeth Engstrom & Susan Stockell—for reading.
Dianna Rodgers—for psychology.

Siren Promised
From Hell

An Introduction
by Simon Clark

A dozen or so years after the publication of *Frankenstein* in 1818, Mary Shelley wrote a new introduction to the 1831 edition. By then *Frankenstein* had already been a huge bestseller, a successful play, and laid the foundation of the monster mythos that continues to prosper today. In that later introduction Mary Shelley wrote this in the new edition of her famous novel: '*And now, once again, I bid my hideous progeny go forth and prosper. I have an affection for it, for it was the offspring of happy days, when death and grief were but words, which found no true echo in my heart.*'

The key words that are relevant not only to Mary Shelley's personal view of her literary creation, but also the book you now hold in your hands, are '*when death and grief were but words, which found no true echo in my heart.*' Mary wrote her book as a young woman. At the time her invented episodes of death, destruction and a man constructed of corpse parts, then brought to life, to ultimately murder its own creator were, she acknowledged, frivolous play things originally intended to amuse herself and her companion during inclement weather at the famous Villa Diodati. By the time she penned the second introduction for a revised *Frankenstein,* her husband was dead and her spirit had been corroded by this and other tragedies great and small. So, in short, the fictional incidents of death and grief that befall Frankenstein and his nameless monster did come to find a true echo in her heart in the face of enduring life as a grieving widow and supporting a father who apparently sucked the financial lifeblood out of her.

I, like most of my fellow horror writers, am in the same position as the young Mary Shelley. We write stories about monsters whether they be vampires, phantoms, demons, zombies, serial killers—the whole uncanny menagerie—and just like the young girl exercising her quill in the Swiss villa, we've never actually encountered our monsters, never mind battled with them. They haven't hurt our families or us. In truth, for most horror writers, our demons are good to us. Our monsters—our *imagined* monsters—pay household bills, they generate royalty checks, cash advances, rights, sales. Our monsters treat us to new DVD players and vacations. Our demons make us happy. And the bottom line is, just like many horror writers, our stories of blood and mayhem are *'the offspring of happy days, when death and grief were but words, which found no true echo in my heart'*—that should read *our* hearts, of course. That's not to say horror writers don't work hard at their craft; nor do we fail to believe in our story's 'artistic' truth. In reality, the demons we manufacture in our minds tend not to torment our families, or us, or generate grief and discord among those who care about us.

Therefore it's an honor for me to write this introduction of *Siren Promised*. It's humbling, too, because it has been created by two people who *have* encountered demons; they *have* suffered what I cannot begin to imagine; they have fought those demons and ultimately, God willing, conquered them. I am, of course, talking about Demon Alcohol and Demon Drug. At the very beginning of the book, both men make the stark acknowledgment: *Alan is an alcoholic. Jeremy is a drug addict.* I daresay both would agree that many of the words contained in *Siren Promised* do find a 'true echo' in their hearts.

Both men wrote the narrative. One of the pair, Alan M. Clark, provided the artwork that succeeds brilliantly in being simultaneously both beautiful and horrifying. *Siren Promised* possesses the veracity of men who have witnessed terrors that most of us can only imagine. I guess, too, that as well as sharing many of those terrors and degradations with us in fiction, it also forms part of a personal weaponry that keeps their own demons at bay and serves as a warning to others.

We read the newspapers, we watch TV, we're familiar with phrases such as 'substance abuse,' 'detox,' 'rehab.' So when we're presented with the story here of twenty-nine-year-old Angie Smith emerging from 'her time in detox hell,' initially it could be an everyday event that occurs repeatedly in just about every neighborhood the world over. To read an account compressed in a few stark lines in a newspaper is to render it almost banal: A story as commonplace as weeds in an overgrown garden. In reality every single story of a battle against drink or drug addiction is an epic struggle of men and women against personal demons. It's every bit as vast and as harrowing as the archetypal hero's battle against legendary monsters found in ancient myth.

Siren Promised is exceptional and compelling. Not solely because both Jeremy Robert Johnson and Alan M. Clark have battled the demons of addiction. It's not only the fact that they experienced the pain and witnessed their loved ones' suffering too; or that they may have encountered crushing setbacks and heartbreaking defeats before winning through. What makes *Siren Promised* such a towering achievement is the rare skill that both men possess to transform their personal experiences into a work of such visionary power. It's harrowing, it's horrific, it's moving, and it's mesmerizing. As a body of words alone, it is an astonishing achievement. With the addition of Alan's unique artwork it is transfigured. It is elevated to a volume that I firmly believe will stand the test of time.

I've been fortunate enough to see Alan's original artwork on display. Those big, bold canvases capture both dream and nightmare. I know I've said it before, but it's worth repeating: those paintings are simultaneously beautiful and disturbing. In equal measures I've been fascinated yet repelled. However, the conviction that overrode an up-welling of genuine emotion as I stared, wide-eyed, at the artwork was that these were works of a truly original talent. One with an uncanny gift to transport us to worlds that we all have visited in our sleep.

So here it is, *Siren Promised*, a consummate body of words and pictures that has the power to carry us to places that I sincerely hope we'll never visit in real life. Places which, I pray *will find no true echo in* our *hearts*. But *Siren Promised* is a 'virtual' journey that is fulfilling, some might add empowering.

Experience it.

Learn from it.

—Simon Clark
Doncaster, England
May 2004

Siren Promised

1—Cypher

Angie Smith had done her time in detox Hell. Her self-imposed exile had ended. Her new life was waiting beyond the border of the bed that had held her like a life raft through terrible, dope-sick storms.

She listened to the sound of her heart beating, a slow and muffled pulse resonating in her ear drums. Her blood's motion and the steady hum of an oscillating fan were the only sounds traveling through the bare, beige and tan room. She took a deep waking breath and sucked up the smell of stale, sweat-soaked sheets, and the thin aroma of coffee drifting in beneath the guest room door. She figured her friend Stacy was up and enjoying breakfast.

Maybe I'll leave this miserable little room today. Have breakfast even. Something besides water and chicken noodle soup.

Her stomach turned at the thought, growling audibly while her belly clenched.

She'd grown used to the sounds of her body in the last three weeks. Detox had a way of making her feel very connected to her flesh, in all the worst ways. Cold-turkey tremors, the frenzied edges of white-knuckle seizures, abdominal cramps, and fevers so bad she felt like her head had been placed in a furnace. Her brain had betrayed her too, subjecting her to long periods of delirium followed by epic stretches of sharp lucidity with nothing to do but hurt. She'd fought back against the pain by repeating her new mantra, her reasons for leaving her old life behind.

Get clean. Get away from Cypher. Get back to Kaya and be her mother.

She knew she could do these things. Every day brought her a step closer. Each night that she saw the sunlight fading through the thin, white sheet that was tacked up over the window, she knew she could do it. She could succeed and make it back to Monahan and be a mother to Kaya before they'd both grown too old; before her thirteen-year-old daughter hated her absolutely.

I'm only twenty-nine. It's not too late. Get clean. Get away from Cypher. Get back to Kaya.

Angie rose slowly from her sagging twin bed, delicately, to avoid passing out. She'd put her body through so much. She felt like she'd been a bunny in a pharmaceutical testing lab, the technicians' voices in her ears. "What happens if we drip LSD in its eyes?" "What will a steady dose of dilaudid do to this creature's heart rate?" Cypher had been behind much of her daily dosing, a lab technician posing as a boyfriend, watching her twitch, studying the results, looking for a way to exert maximum control.

Fuck him. Fuck me for letting him do that to me. I'm done with him, with that whole part of my life. I'd have been dead in a couple of years if I stayed with him. If he finds me, I might be dead anyway.

Angie shook off goosebumps and bent down to pick up an extra large t-shirt from the soft, shag carpet beneath her feet. She ran her hands through her tangled, shoulder-length black hair and sighed.

Back to the real world, I guess.

Her stomach rumbled again, begging her to eat.

Okay, okay. I'll have some breakfast and then I can talk to Stacy about maybe borrowing some cash and getting home.

She pictured home. She pictured Kaya there, waiting for her mother's arrival, sitting on the front step. Her daughter would smile when she saw her mom, her *new* mom, all cleaned up and sparkling and ready to be a mother. *At last.* They'd hug forever, and Angie would bend down and smell Kaya's hair and kiss the thin line where it parted down the middle, and Kaya would hug her tighter, and everything could start again.

Better this fantasy than the ones Angie used to have, imagining countless deaths, accidental and premeditated, for her daughter. Angie was never the cause of death in these fantasies, but at the end of each car accident or drowning, she'd feel a terrible release, a freedom from responsibility. Her new point of view would not allow such thoughts.

Lately she even had a kind thought for her mother, Colleen. Although Angie despised the woman, she could imagine thanking her for being there and looking after Kaya all these years.

After that Angie'd have her whole life ahead of her. Maybe ballet lessons with Kaya, mother and daughter spinning gracefully together. They could gently tend to each other's sore feet after a long day of floating on air.

They could cook dinner together, and after eating they could splash each other with dishwater while standing at the sink, side by side.

They could fall asleep together on the nights when Kaya needed her to be close.

Angie rose from the bed, stretched out her arms, and managed a smile. Morning sun fell across her pale skin and warmed her to the coming day.

"You want me to go to an outdoor rave? Tonight, seriously?"

"Yeah, Angie. You deserve a little bit of fun. You've been milling around the house acting useless for a couple of days now, even though you say you're feeling much better. You should get out, avoid cabin fever, re-socialize yourself before you head home. So yeah, I'm serious."

"Stacy, I don't even know if I want to leave the house right now." She took a sip of hot, black coffee and tried not to look pathetic. She wanted to appear strong for Stacy, to show that she hadn't taken Angie in and helped her through her detox for nothing.

"Angie, you've got to get out at some point...."

"I know. But a *rave*? Isn't your twelve step shit against that?"

"Kind of. But I don't take that stuff as gospel. I'm into moderation. I mean, if we don't celebrate now and then, what are we fighting for anyway? You've always liked to dance. Are you going to tell me that you only listened to music and danced in the past because you were high?"

Angie looked at Stacy across the small, round kitchen table. There didn't seem to be any kind of malice in her face, any threat. Stacy leaned in closer to Angie, cinnamon on her breath.

"Listen, Angie, you're my girl, you know? And I'm not sure, once you leave this place, that I'll ever see you again. It's probably smart if you never come back here. So just go out there with me tonight. They've got like twelve DJ's and the party is at this tree farm out by the old Chandler swamps. It's gonna be sick. We'll stay sober, we'll dance, we'll walk around in the trees and talk, like we used to do before you met that piece of shit. It'll just be us and some dope beats, and maybe we smoke a bowl or two and just chill. Please, Angie?"

"Okay, but if I don't dig it, we bail, right?"

"Right."

"Okay. Okay... fuck it. I'll go. I deserve to have some fun."

Stay clean. Get away from Cypher. Get home to Kaya.

Right after this.

Angie was vibrating with excitement as she walked the dirt trail to the bass-slammed epicenter of the party. She adored the feeling of the balmy evening air on her skin, a gift from the strange, very late Indian Summer that had settled into the area weeks after the trees had shed the last of their Fall leaves.

The party itself was in full swing by the time they arrived at about 2 AM. Angie looked at the mass of twisting, colorful people dancing like little pagans before the speaker-gods and decided she'd made the right choice. She loved to dance and was nearly shaking, eager to run right into the maelstrom and feel her body move with the music. She wondered how strong she would feel now, how long she could dance without any coke or pills.

I don't care how I feel. I'll dance until my body quits. Stacy will have to cart me home crippled.

Angie and Stacy quickly found a prime spot down by the front right speaker banks, just to the side of the DJ table. They danced side by side, facing the relentless onslaught of sound coming from the speakers. The bass was vibrating so strongly that Angie felt it moving the hairs on her arms.

She looked over at Stacy, who was smiling a wide, white-toothed grin and hopefully feeling the same way. Angie looked to the sky above and kept smiling, feeling her legs trace graceful arcs beneath her.

Her pulse raced naturally, avoiding the jackrabbit palpitations that used to make her vomit when she was faded on E. She pushed herself to keep moving, all smiles and sweat and motion.

Anybody watching me right now probably figures I'm rolled to the high heavens.

Angie didn't care. She wasn't dancing for other people. She was dancing for herself, for the life she was building from the ground up.

For my future.

Her body felt incredibly light as she danced. She moved among the other dancers with her eyes closed, feeling holy, untouchable. She imagined herself borne on wings, swirling night under her skin, lightning crashing around her as the music kept her afloat.

After an hour of dancing, she had stopped sweating. She was burning up. Her mouth was desert-dry, and she realized she needed to get a glass of water or juice or anything so she could keep going, keep dancing.

She turned away from the speaker, toward the crowd behind her.

Stacy was nowhere to be seen.

And Cypher was right behind her, smiling, watching her, with his arms crossed in front of his chest, nodding his head with the beat.

She tried to look into his eyes, unsure of how to react, wondering if she should just follow her gut reaction and run.

Why does he have to be here tonight? Jesus. Why tonight? This is my party. He's probably just dealing. He can't even dance.

Cypher took a step closer, the muscles in his slender arms twitching as he dropped them to his sides. His brown eyes were hidden in his sockets, shaded black and empty by the moonlight. He ran his hands over his neatly shaved head and looked her up and down.

"Hey, Angie. Where you been all my life?"

Angie looked around, comforted by the dancing masses that thronged her and Cypher. Witnesses. She couldn't see Stacy anywhere.

Probably off making out with some guy with a cleft chin. She loves cleft chins. Why isn't she here right now, watching my back? She's the one with the pepper spray.

"Hey, Angie, what's up with the silent treatment?"

He looked strangely relaxed, and Angie was hoping he'd popped some peaceful pills tonight, something that would make him easier to deal with.

"Nothing's going on, Cyph. Just chilling out, dancing. You?"

"Me? I'm just watching you, thinking about how much better you'd look wearing nothing, dancing like you used to do for me."

"Yeah, Cyph, like back in the good old days—that's over, Cypher."

She felt strong. She felt right saying it, and registered the shock in his face. She said it again.

"It's over, Cypher."

He paused and then began to laugh. He looked her over while he laughed, his eyes oozing ownership. *"It's over, Angie? It's over? I don't remember us ever deciding on that. So fuck you."*

"What?"

"Yeah, fuck you for running from me. Fuck you for leaving me alone. You think things are easy without you?"

He didn't really need her. She knew better than that. She'd seen him with other girls. Still, the need in his voice *felt* real.

No. Remember. Get away from Cypher. Remember how he is, how he treats you. Get away.

She turned to walk away, to move past the speaker banks and use the crowd to block his movement. Then she could find Stacy and they could get the hell out....

His hand was tight on her right arm. She tried to pull away. He was too strong for her. Dancing for an hour after doing three week's detox had left her frail.

Then *he* was leading her, pulling her past the same speaker banks she'd wanted to hide behind. His free hand reached into his pocket and swung quickly up to his mouth.

Angie hoped that whatever he was swallowing was poison. That he would drop dead and leave her alone and let her get out of here and back to her daughter, where she should be right this minute.

They were behind the speaker banks when he pulled her body up to his. He whispered to her, sadness in his voice that she couldn't pin down as a lie. "Angie, please, just make things right and kiss me, *just kiss me*, and then we can go dance, and I'll let you go your way and never see you again."

Angie struggled against him, but did not scream. She felt a sick affection for him that she couldn't shake when he was directly in front of her, looking into her eyes. Her mind swam, overwhelmed.

What if I don't... I mean, what will he do to me? He's too strong. I don't know... Maybe he will let me go. Fuck... I....

She kissed him. Their dry lips met; his tongue pushed into her mouth, deep, running over the surface of her own as she recoiled.

She recognized the sting in her mouth instantly. She'd had enough acid before tonight.

He'd just kissed her with a mouth full of liquid L.

She was dosed and wrapped in Cypher's arms.

She pushed away from him. He let go and began laughing. She fell backwards and landed on her ass in the hard dirt.

"Oh, shit, Angie... you should see the look on your face. Fucking priceless."

She turned and ran back into the crowd, expecting to feel his hands on her body again, ready to cry for help. As she crossed the dance area she looked back over her shoulder and caught no sight of Cypher.

Stacy was also nowhere to be seen. Her friend was vapor, the big disappearance of the night.

Angie knew she didn't have long before the doses hit her system. Liquid always caught her quick and stealth-silent. She had mere minutes until her brain betrayed her and left her defenseless.

I'm like an animal hit with a tranquilizer dart. Cypher's probably watching me, waiting for me to collapse, hoping my brain sizzles.

Once I'm high, he can get in. In to me. Into my head. He always does.

Angie yelled for Stacy, but no one was paying attention. The party was in full swing. People yelled things just to hear their voices intermingled with the waves of music that pummeled the crowd. Her noise was just flotsam in a shipwreck of sound.

She had reached the outside edge of the dance area and was headed toward the trail leading out and away from the party, hoping she could hitch a ride out with anybody but Cypher.

Then the acid hit, a shard of chemical shrapnel deep in her brain.

She stopped in her tracks and stared at the scene ahead of her. Part of her brain kept asserting itself. *It's not real, it's not real, it's not real.*

But she knew what she was seeing.

Angie *knew* that both of the kids making out by the white van were dead. They had to be. Pieces of them were falling off. They didn't notice.

Angie stood a few feet away and watched as the boy's tongue surged into the girl's mouth and tore through the skin on her right cheek, leaving part of her face flapping loose in the wind that swept through the woods surrounding them. The boy's arm atrophied into a reed-thin stick as his hand reached up for the girl's breast.

The girl turned toward Angie. Her eyes were melting, dripping down her cheeks, viscous and gleaming in the strobe lights that flashed repetitive by the DJ booth.

Angie looked away and tried to keep her deep-fried fast food dinner from relocating. Her stomach burned.

Fucking BAD acid. No doubt. Bathtub brewed strychnine bullshit for sure. What has he done to me?

She ran her shaking hands through her dark, greasy hair, tried to remember to breathe and slow her heart beat down. She couldn't. Her blood pump was on overdrive.

Maybe. It could just be the acid talking.

"If it's not the acid," she thought, "then I'll be waking up in the hospital again."

She shuddered, remembering the last time she'd awakened to the stark white, clinical surroundings of St. David. Her mind flashed on the tubes they put into her, forcing her to stay alive. For a moment she felt the tube running down her throat again. She gagged. The world swam purple-green in front of her. She wondered where Cypher was, if he had followed her and was watching her stumble through the party, waiting to catch her alone.

And then what?

She turned her head to the sky and tried to shake it clear. The scraggly tops of bark-stripped water ash trees shivered and blurred together, vibrating silhouettes backlit by a full moon with an acid induced rainbow-corona around it.

She heard a gas-driven generator rattling in the distance, over-whelmed by the constant, propulsive sounds of hard techno coming from the sound system.

The bass pounded, relentless, over and over again, past the point of being tribal. It was rhythm turned sinister, the heartbeat of overheated reptiles trapped in mechanical wombs, being primed with adrenaline, waiting to tear into the flesh of whatever stood before them.

She shuddered again, hearing the music, feeling separate from it and isolated even though there were hundreds of other kids at the party.

Kids. Angie wondered if she really counted herself as a kid anymore. Shit, she was a year short of thirty, still wearing a baby tee, a too-short skirt and dirty gray platform sneaks. The costume had worked for her in the past. She had found she could still get fourteen-year-olds to trust her enough to share some ketamine rails or a joint.

Her thoughts became dangerously random. She had difficulty focusing on any one thought with urgency. "I've got to find Stacy... got to get out of here... I need a weapon... something... maybe if I smoke some weed it'll calm this acid down."

She had a hard time focusing on the danger that Cypher posed. Instead it was the thought of a cloud of smoke that got Angie moving, walking awkward on the uneven earthen floor of the forest.

Jesus, my brain's going soft. I've got to get out of here. I just don't....

She fluctuated between terror and a feeling of strange, euphoric safety that said things were going to be okay. That this was still *her* party.

Maybe Cypher really is going to leave me alone. Maybe I can find Stacy and we can find something to calm me down, and then we can roll out of here. I just need something to chill out this acid a little bit. Something to help me walk straight and master my high. Maybe some oxycons.

Just the word *oxycons*, and she felt a shiver of pleasure up her spine.

You're just like your mother sometimes, huh, sweetie? Shouldn't you be leaving?

God, she hated that voice inside her head, acid-amplified and shrill. The voice that wanted to make her think too much.

Shouldn't you be getting home to Kaya? You're not safe here.
"Shut up!" Angie shouted, and the voice in her head seemed to register it. She knew she needed to control the fear. The voice was quiet now, but there were still bad acid visions and belly aches and the constant pulsing sound of music devolving into a steady four/four stomp. Her eyes drifted to the swampy woods around her.

Angie walked faster, determined to find Stacy, and *now*.
Stacy will help me.

Angie walked quickly, past the surging speakers and light-saturated dance floor. She brushed against a sweaty shirtless guy with a pacifier in his mouth, almost tripping over his gigantic yellow pants. She stopped and looked around. No Stacy anywhere. Her brain caught flashes, bits and pieces in the stimulus storm. Tongues sliding over each other, Virginia Slims being smoked by slouching girls in tank tops, glowsticks drawing figure eights over and over again, dreads throwing sweat, glitter in the hair on a man's back, a boy with cystic acne jamming a Vicks inhaler into his right nostril, a girl seated on the ground Indian style, throwing up into her own cupped hands and smiling.

It was too much. Angie closed her eyes and cursed Cypher for forcing this on her.

Gravity felt tight on her spine, pulling her toward the ground. She had that weird feeling that everything would be okay if she'd just lie down on the ground. The acid in her skull threw a vision to the front of her closed eyes.

There I am, half buried in the ground. People are walking on me, over me. I'm not there. They don't care. Wooden roots have replaced my eyes and are intertwined, twisting around each other before they push into the dirt. My mouth is wide open and full of soil.

She screamed again, a base level shriek. The people dancing around her gave wide berth.

No one asked if she was okay. It was like she didn't exist. She was ether. No, less than that. Ether could kill. People gave a shit about that.

She was surrounded and alone, and Cypher was out there, somewhere in the party, laughing at her.

Angie grabbed the boy in the oversized yellow pants, then held up her right hand in front of him.

"Please touch my hand. Prove to me I'm real."

He smirked. Angie read the look on his face. It said, "You are a burnout." Crystal clear and loud, this judgment from a kid wearing a plush Pokemon backpack.

She stared at her hand, watched his finger approaching her flesh.

Her vision blurred, she felt another strychnine twinge in her belly.

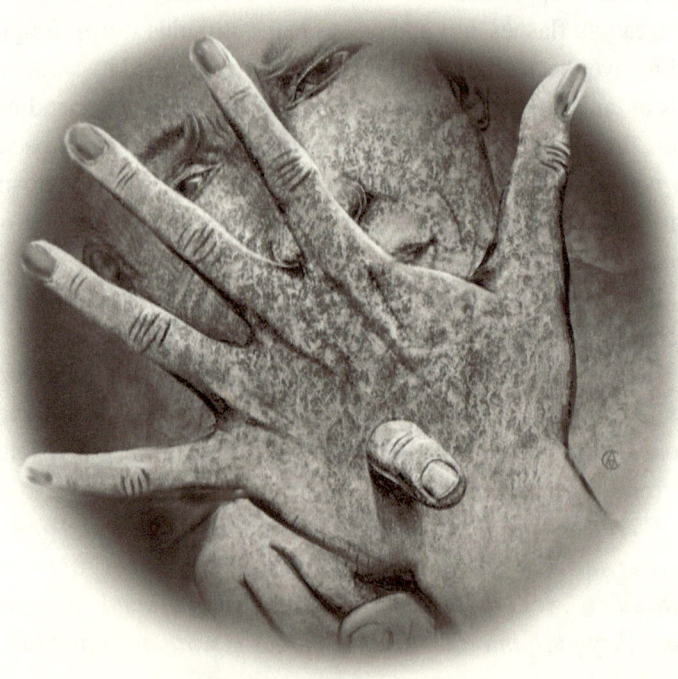

She watched his finger push right through the middle of her hand.

She bleached white, pulled away, and shrieked in the kid's face, fear on her breath.

He laughed at her and kept dancing.

His laugh echoed in the trees around them. She heard the trees join in, low laughter rasping from their brushing branches, a whisper.

You're one of us.

She tasted soil in her mouth and tried to spit it out. She couldn't conjure enough saliva to erase the taste.

She walked away from the dance area and back toward the dark of the woods, approaching a strip of yellow tape strung from tree to tree that marked off the swamp/farm boundaries. DO NOT CROSS.

"Hey, Angie, where you goin', bitch?"

The voice was too deep to be Stacy's. It sounded like boiling motor oil.

It was Cypher, doubtless. He always managed to be around when she was collapsing. It was his gift. Angie looked around and realized there were no other partiers within twenty feet of them.

He'd waited for her to stray from the herd.

"Hey, I'm talking to you. Fucking talk back."

Angie lifted her head, just grateful that someone was talking to her. It meant she existed. That was all she'd really wanted in the past, to exist. She hadn't wanted much more and rarely tried to do anything but finish up a day, and then the next. And if people like Cypher helped the day go a little faster, then all the better.

But Cypher doesn't want to help me right now. He wants to hurt me. Doesn't he? And I don't just want to exist anymore. I want to be with Kaya. I want to be her mom.

Don't I? Jesus, what's going on?

Her voice came out thin, distant. "I don't know where I'm going, Cypher. I need help." The sentence forced its way out of her mouth and felt like resignation.

"You need help, Angie? I got that right here." He opened his arms like a patron saint and laughed. The sound made Angie picture Cypher as a kid. There he is, bashing a cat's head into a sidewalk. Over, and over.

Angie staggered forward, fell into Cypher's bony arms, pressed against his flat, amphetamine hyper chest.

"There, baby, now we're spending some real quality time together."

He leaned his head down and kissed her forehead. His lips were chapped, cracked. She felt the dead skin brush her hairline.

"I mean, did you think I'm just gonna kick around solo all night while you trip the fucking light fantastic out in Sherwood Forest, cause if you think that, you're on some real fucking bullshit, like more than ever. We got a history together, right? You know what I'm sayin'?"

He wrapped his arms around her tighter and squeezed the breath from her. He sighed heavy. His breath smelled like Jack Daniel's and bad fish.

"Hey, Cypher? The acid is too much...it's just...too much...nothing's making sense."

"Not my fault you've gone soft. You used to be my little acid superstar and now you're telling me you can't handle your shit?"

He was amped; she could sense it. He was acting like he'd been tweeking for days. He'd shed his calm dance floor demeanor and gone simian. When he was like this she had to play it whispers and tiptoes with him. It was easy to fuck up and push him over his edge. She could feel him waiting for that push, begging for an excuse to put her in another cast... or worse. She knew of something that would chill both of them out, and maybe let her dream away the poison he'd kissed into her bloodstream.

"Hey, you got any oxycons?"

"Naw, Angie, we ate all those last week. They're gone as gone can be, you know? It's like we floated off that cloud a long time ago. It's your fault, too. You get greedy off that shit and just shut the fuck down and stare at the ceiling like its all you ever wanted and I get bored and watch TV. Fuck them oxycons, man, you just get boring off 'em. I do have some shit though, if you want to be a fucking rock star."

Rock star.

Shit.

Angie wanted whatever would shut the acid down. If she had to blaze it out with some crack, could she?

She could still taste soil in her mouth. The trees were whispering to her. This trip had to end.

"Yeah, Cypher, load it up."

"Yeah, Cypher, load it up?" His voice was high pitched, mocking. "What, you startin' to think we're little buddies and shit? You think this shit is free? You think you can just drop into my arms, fried out of your fucking mind, and I'll let you smoke the last of my yay for nothing? For nothing?"

It's never for nothing, is it, sweetie?

"No, Cyph, I can hook you up, too."

"Fucking right. You promise?"

"Yeah, Cyph."

"Let's go then. I got the shit in my dash, back at the ride."

She walked with him, felt the evening get colder and goosebumps cover her body as they walked out toward his Accord parked on an old, isolated logging trail by the party.

What am I doing? I should run. I should run and find Stacy or a DanceSafe booth or anybody that might help. I can't go back to this. I've run this pattern for years. It's been killing me.

Still, Angie followed. She felt like she was watching herself from inside her skull.

Cypher reached his car, cracked open his door, and grabbed a plastic vial from his dash. He loaded up the pipe and pulled a butane lighter out of his console.

"Shit, Cyph, no torch? You want me to butane this shit?"

She didn't know why she was pressing his buttons, watching his blood pressure rise. Her words left her mouth without emotion, and felt hollow and separate, uncontrolled. Dangerous.

"Listen, Angie, I can go ahead and smoke all this by my lonely and you can watch me and bug out and talk to God and Buddha and whoever else is probably floating in the sky above your fried little head. If that's what you want then go ahead and say it. If not, shut the fuck up and help me out."

Whispers and moans came from the woods, from the space between the trees, and crawled into her ear.

It's quiet here. So quiet. You won't be alone. There are others here.

She felt her lips moving, slow and rhythmic, with the whispers that entered her mind. She felt cold inside, ice-razors in her belly.

She considered Cypher's proposition.

She remained silent. She needed a way out. He had it in his hands.

She walked closer to him, put her hand to his crotch. He was hard already. He knew which way she'd answer. She hated him for it, hated herself even more.

She knew there was no time for romance. With Cypher there never had been. What she wanted right now was someone to kiss her, to talk to her, to trace lips across her belly and kiss the little rose tattoo just above her right breast. But that wasn't going to happen. This wasn't love. This was a transaction.

He turned her around and lifted her skirt. She looked back at him and feigned a smile. It was all teeth, no eyes.

He didn't notice the manufactured grin. He was hitting the pipe, taking a deep, hot lungful and then shaking, the high immediate and vital.

She pushed her underwear down to the curve behind her knees and reached back for the pipe and lighter. He pushed himself into her, rough, before she even took her first hit. He moved his hips steady, pounding with the inescapable four/four beat that reverberated through the tupelos and cyrilla trees around them.

She put the flame to the bowl, breathed as deep as she could, pulled hard, and felt her heart explode in her chest, hitting hummingbird speed in a split second. She was dry down south, and

Cypher was tearing the shit out of her, but her hit wiped everything out for a moment, a cool perfect moment where dawn was just seconds away and the sunshine was waiting to wrap her up in warmth and hold her, curled up, forever.

Then she felt sick again, ice in her belly causing a nauseating ache, and she was pulled right back into her body, being dry-fucked.

Her gut ruptured and the burger and fries she ate for dinner burst from her mouth and sprayed the top of Cypher's car while he grunted behind her, whispering a sick monologue, calling her a dirty little bitch and a worthless cunt and telling her that this time he was going to bust so big that she'd have to have another kid scraped, and it was all too much for Angie, and she held back another heave in her belly and throat and put the pipe to her lips again and put the lighter to it and there it was again, that feeling that the world was okay, and the one hand she had pressed against the roof of the car slid in her puke and she slipped forward and off of Cypher.

She was barely inside of her own body. Her pulse defined everything; two hundred beats per minute, burning up every inch of her. She was beginning to convulse when Cypher grabbed her hips, struggling to get back inside her. She tried to reach the pipe, but she had dropped it somehow and things weren't going right, and now all she held was the lighter.

She was staring at the little plastic lighter and trying hard to breathe when Cypher spit on her asshole and forced himself in.

"*No,*" she cried, and the pain focused her, but her body remained immobile. Cypher had done this before, but was never so brutal.

"Shut up, bitch," Cypher said. "You need this." He gripped her right arm and twisted it up behind her back.

Move! Do something! Make it stop hurting!

She couldn't, no matter how many times the voice in her head demanded it; her body just wouldn't respond. Was it paralysis as self-defense? He would beat her to unconsciousness if she denied him.

Where was Stacy? Where was Angie, the Angie she woke up

inside of this morning, full of promise?

She could feel so much. The white fire at the base of her spine. The deep ache as her right shoulder strained to pop from the socket. The warm blood and spit running down the inside of her thighs. Her heart straining against its own fibers, threatening to give at any moment. Her teeth grinding. Her mind shutting down.

Letting go.

Getting out, out of this, out of everything. Going, maybe, to the sun.

She thought of the sun, but she felt winter on her face, cold to the point of numbing her skin. The feeling was coming from her left, along the tree line.

Angie turned her head toward the blackness of the swamp.

Her daughter, Kaya, was there, standing at the edge of the woods, shimmering. Waving at her.

Watching her.

Angie could see through Kaya, see the branches of the trees swaying behind her, but she was still *there*, waving to her mom, glowing soft in her overalls and pig-tails. She was holding her arms out as if to embrace Angie through the distance and woods between them.

Angie felt her lips moving again, heard a voice coming from her mouth that was not her own. It couldn't be. She didn't own the words.

You don't have to be alone. She is with us. Go to her.

Angie tasted earth and loam on her tongue. The heaviness of it in her mouth and throat brought her back into her body, her pain soaring as Cypher slammed steady into her and split her open again and again.

Join her. She needs you. She's so cold.

Okay. I can hold her and warm her up and kiss her and then we can let go and we won't need anymore. We won't need anything. Anybody.

I'm coming, Kaya.

"Stop," she shouted to Cypher.

He twisted her arm tighter.

Angie reached back with her left hand and tried to push Cypher out of her and off of her. He twisted her arm even tighter and pushed deeper and harder. Her left shoulder smashed into the front right window of his car. Her right shoulder, twisted too far, popped out of its socket, with the sound of glass crunching in a paper bag. Her left hand gripped his butane lighter tight.

She reached back, pushed the lighter as far as she could between her legs, and ignited it.

She heard Cypher screaming, and it felt right to her. She clenched herself tight around him and held him there, the fire searing and blackening his balls, burning through the skin.

He punched his left fist down, hard, at the base of her back, and then slipped out of her. He fell to the dirt and curled up, cradling his groin in his hands as smoke whisped through his fingers.

Angie slid off the car, her breath fogging his window as she collapsed. She hit the ground hard and her right shoulder popped back into its socket. She leaned on her left hand to stand up.

Then she was walking, and moving toward the morass past the woods, where her daughter was waiting for her.

She followed the little girl into the woods.

I'm coming.

She could hear Cypher yelling. She guessed most people at the party could hear him by now, his voice hoarse and guttural, screaming over and over. She had to push further into the woods, into some kind of quiet. Away from what had just happened.

The woods always felt quiet to her. Quiet like a prayer. Quiet like death. Perfect, space without sound, aside from the wind.

The shape of her daughter was fifty yards ahead, and moving into the inky black woods.

If I lose sight of her, what will I do? Where will I go?

Kaya began to move faster and further away. Angie followed her for hundreds of yards, far beyond the thin plastic strips reading DO NOT CROSS.

Even with her platform shoes elevating her, the silty black

swamp water occasionally reached Angie's ankles. Sawgrass sliced her skin, paper-thin cuts in her calves that seeped blood.

She followed the shape of her daughter into a gully, grabbing onto the cracked, exposed roots of fever-trees as she stepped down. The roots felt strange in her hands, fleshy and warm.

Angie followed the dim light of her distant daughter to the end of the gully where it gave way to standing water. She ignored the mosquitoes that swarmed her.

Here at the gully's end, the wind felt sharper across her face. She became lightheaded. Branches and debris, like corpses, were hung in the gnarled trees which rose from the water. The trees were old and sparse and reached to the sky like the withered hands of old men.

Angie back-tracked along the gully until she came to a dead end. Static interference ran across her eyes. Angie's skin had gone past numb; her body a heavy sack around her. Her legs gave out beneath her. Her knees went liquid and she hit the ground with a muffled thump.

Angie cried out, "Kaya."

The glowing little girl was nowhere to be seen.

Angie was deep in the woods, bleeding and alone in the dark. Her daughter had left her. Angie felt she deserved it.

How many times have you left her, sweetie?

The truth of the thought and the sick impact of the night hit her full force. Tears fell from Angie's face and dripped across her right forearm, which was trapped under her head as she rolled onto her side.

Angie felt a sudden pain, like tiny needles across her chest and her arm, like the thorns of her rose tattoo had become substance and were pressing through the surface. The trees above her were whispering again.

You are with us now. You can end here. Don't hurt anymore.

She mouthed the words softly without thinking them, her voice devoid of tone. She felt the cold inside her belly spreading across her whole body, interrupted only by the fire in her chest and arms.

Then she felt fear, for a moment, a great and cold blackness that rushed through her and forced reality into her mind, panic-fast.

I'm hallucinating. I'm muttering suicidal bullshit. I can't control any of this. Something is doing this to me. Somebody is fucking with my head.

The little girl couldn't have been Kaya, she was too young. Someone or something had tricked her into being where she was right now, ready to die.

Or maybe you want this, sweetie? It feels right, doesn't it? Dying like this.

No, I have to find Kaya. Get back to Kaya. Make things right.

Yet she was here with the brambles, broken sticks and dead wood in a clearing where nothing grew. She had come to a place where things ended, and she was sinking into the earth.

Maybe Kaya's dead. Maybe it was Kaya's ghost that led me here, revenge for the dreams I used to have about her dying. Maybe one of those dreams wasn't just a dream. But I never meant them, those thoughts, those ideas. I couldn't stomach them. I hated them. I just couldn't stop thinking I'd be free without her. But I never meant it—I was going back for her. I wanted a new life. I wanted to make things right with her.

Fresh pain pulled her from her thoughts. Her arms and chest felt like they were on fire. She lifted her head to see the damage.

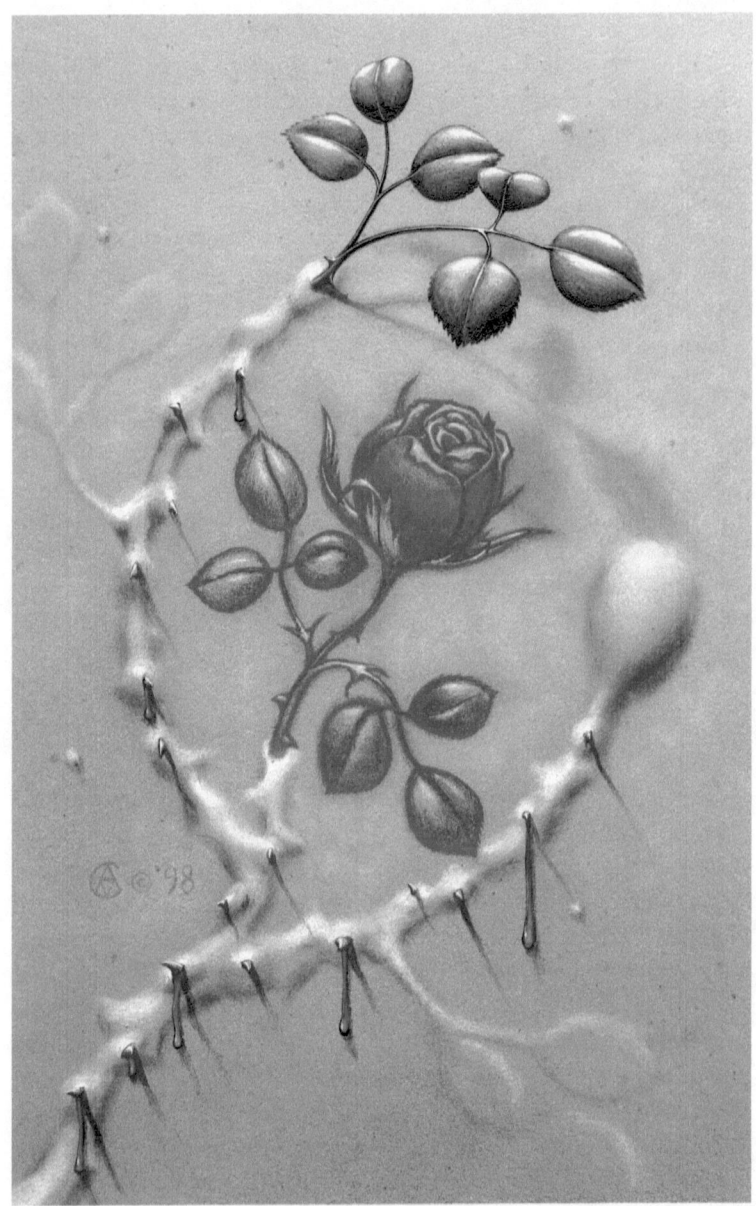

Her arm was burning, held tight to the soil beneath it. The ground was wet with her tears. Something thin and dark was wrapping itself around the *inside* of her right arm, shifting like worms beneath the surface, and the muscle all around it was constricted.

In the thin blue light of the moon she watched as the dark ink growths became thick and spread under the skin of her arm, coming down from her shoulder and branching. She felt them stretching out beneath her skin, spreading from their source. The tendrils wove beneath the skin of her hand.

She looked closer. *Ink. It looks like ink. Dark black and green like the tattoo on my chest.*

The fire beneath her skin soared. She closed her eyes and clenched her jaw to stifle the pain. She heard her skin tearing.

She was blooming.

Roots grew through the skin of her arm, wet with her blood. As the roots pushed into the earth and she sank deeper into the soil, she felt herself connecting to something. Something cold and ancient that wanted her to be still and never move again. Through her new roots, whispers entered her blood, heavy like opium.

Don't be afraid. You can end now. All of you end like this. All of you.

The thorns of the rose pushed through her thin skin and rivulets of blood trickled warm into the ground.

She watched as the ink slithered and coalesced on the back of her hand, creating a perfectly crafted rose bud. She watched the bud swell beneath her skin and then it was pushed out the ends of her fingers and burst into the open, splattering her face with tiny red droplets. All the tendrils emerged into the open and began to rise into the air.

The bud opened in the moonlight, red velvet flower petals dripping with life.

Angie smelled roses, sweet as summer, exhaled, and fell into darkness.

2—Family Time

Colleen wants me to be part of the family now, Curtis Loew thought, choosing another black and white photo to work on. *Why else would she entrust her photo albums to me?*

Well...okay, she doesn't really know I have them. But I'm sure she'd be fine with it.

Having these photo albums, being in charge of repairing and restoring them—it's like I'm the head of the family.

Curtis brushed the long hair out of his eyes and turned the photo over. "I had a cousin Josh Tosent in 1957," he said, delighted, as he retraced the faded name and date on the back of it. Then he turned it over again and looked at the picture of the tall bald man leaning against the Chevy with the giant fins. "I wonder if he's still alive. I'd like a visit with him."

Maybe I'll find him online. Curtis reached over and turned on his computer.

Yes, he was sure Colleen already considered him part of the Smith family. He could even imagine taking care of her in her old age, which would probably not be long in coming. She'd be ill-tempered. She would stink and he'd have to clean her, change her diapers and so on. He wouldn't mind because she was family and that was a bond worth working for. He could put up with a lot if he knew he had a place in her life.

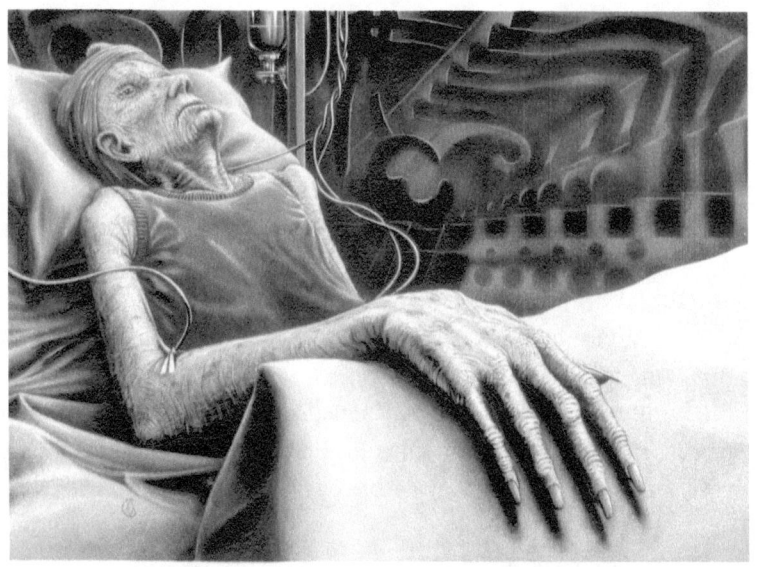

He thought of Kaya Smith playing in the street yesterday in her leotards. He could clearly see the shapes of her breasts and nipples through the fabric. He was certain her grandmother would not talk to her about sex. It looked like he'd have to be the one to do it. Of course it was better if a female family member talked with her, but Colleen...? Poor woman. Well now that he was family, he'd just have to take up the slack.

First he'd have to get Kaya to trust him. *All in good time*, he told himself, trying to relax and let nature take its course. *All in good time*.

Curtis was frustrated with his progress with Kaya. She was not responsive to him. She didn't consider him family yet. He had asked her to call him Uncle Curtis. He had given her gifts: electronic games, a cell phone, even jewelry. It was cheap jewelry that he'd bought at a convenience store, but he was fairly certain it was silver. She'd given him a simple *thank you* with no evidence of emotion behind it.

A couple weeks ago he took Kaya and Colleen out for pizza, but once again Kaya showed no real gratitude. The only time she showed any emotion was when their order came and she discovered there were onions on it.

"You said no onions!" she gasped, her eyes wide and unbelieving. Fearfully, she backed away from the table, looking about helplessly. It would seem the whole world was against her and she didn't know which way to turn.

Curtis felt he had somehow betrayed her, but this passed quickly.

"It'll be *fine*," Colleen said, drunkenly.

"I'll take it back and get another," Curtis said.

"I won't eat here," Kaya said, tears streaming down her cheeks. "I'm going to sit at the window."

Curtis recognized the threat immediately. No one sat out in the open in a public place ever since the spree killings had begun—too many snipers. Children Kaya's age were especially warned about this.

What fascinated Curtis was that her display not only made her more attractive to him, but also stimulated his desire to protect her. Had she learned to do this or did it come naturally? Living with Colleen, Kaya's world was terribly unstable, perhaps even dangerous. But the outburst was obviously not for her grandmother—Colleen had long since stopped caring about Kaya's emotional reactions. Would she have done this with anyone, or had it been especially for Curtis' benefit? If the latter were true, perhaps she did have feelings for him. Perhaps she did see him as a member of the fam-ily after all: The strong male figure who would protect and provide for her. Perhaps she was testing this bond.

I suppose this is what it's like, dealing with your children, Curtis thought.

"We'll just leave," he said with a smile. "Go get in the car. I'll pay up and be right out."

Kaya was immediately calmed.

Curtis waited for the door to close behind the two Smiths, then ordered another pizza—*without onions*—to be delivered to Colleen's house. Then he drove them home and waited in his car until they had retreated indoors. He knew Colleen would fix Kaya a dinner of egg sandwiches. This was a standard meal she fixed nearly every night of the week and their house stank of it. He hoped the pizza would arrive before Colleen could get that done.

His computer ready, Curtis connected to the internet. He used a search engine to look for Josh Tosent with no results. Since he was missing cousin Josh so much, he decided he'd just have to invent something about him. But as he steered his browser to the genealogy site he'd been using to help him build a family tree for the Smiths, he decided that perhaps he shouldn't invent anything for cousin Josh just yet. If little was known of his family in general, that branch of the tree might be just the one on which to graft the small twig he had built to contain his own name.

He searched information about the Tosent family in general and found several pedigrees that had been posted, including one which mentioned Josh Tosent as the son of one Harold Pulwart Tosent, adopted son of Randall Henson Smith, Colleen's grandfather. Apparently little was known of Harold's origins. There was no information about where the name Tosent—presumably his father's name—had come from. Harold Pulwart Tosent had had two children, cousin Josh Folger Tosent and Elloise James Tosent. There was no further information about Elloise, but that she had headed to California in the '60s and was never heard from again. There was speculation that she had died in an automobile accident at the age of twenty-two.

This was just the kind of set-up Curtis had hoped for. He found he could download the pedigree. Now he could alter it, adding the name he had come up with for his father, Gerald Troy Loew, as being the husband to Elloise James Tosent. He did this and then uploaded it to appear on his web site. He'd post a interest-piquing note—something like, "Newly discovered Tosent-Loew connection to Smith family"—on the message board forum he'd found belonging to the Smiths to whom Colleen and Kaya were related, and provide a link to his site.

Now he's my *Uncle* Josh, Curtis thought. Satisfied that he had legitimized his membership in the Smith family, Curtis disconnected from the internet and shut down his computer, then went to bed.

He dreamed of Kaya. A naked angel, she hovered over him.
There were eyes all around them.
Curtis felt guilty as hell.

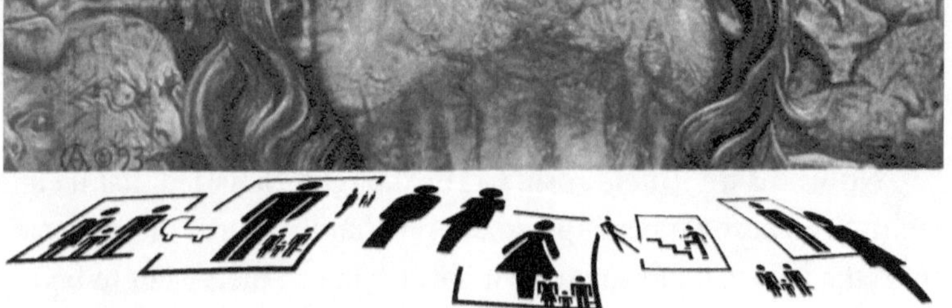

3—Sunrise, Sunset

One drop.

Then another.

Then the clouds broke wide and the rain began.

Angie could feel it happening. She knew the rain was pouring down and felt it soaking through the soil and into her body. She heard the steady percussion of each drop hitting the ground by her head. She could *see* the rain falling all around her, but not with her eyes. It was as though her optic nerves had rooted themselves to the ground and she had an impossible view of the gully, one which was all-encompassing and not limited by line of sight.

She could feel the rain dropping into her wide-open eyes and covering her vision as if with a veil of tears, but she didn't blink because her lids were obstructed from closing.

She didn't move at all.

She couldn't.

Angie felt the drops run into her gaping mouth, a tiny river of coppery water sliding down her throat. Stranger was the sensation that the water was entering through her arm where the rose had taken root. The hand beneath the rose looked stiff, its fingers splayed wide, claw-like. The fingertips looked slimmer, bonier, like her flesh was being sucked out and down into the earth through the same roots that fed her.

This isn't real. This is just the acid. It won't let me go. I'm probably in the hospital again, hooked to machines, pissing through a tube. Cypher's standing in the corner, laughing, waiting for me to wake up.

The sun that had crested the trees just moments before was now beginning its descent. She tracked its light. It shimmered through the rain as it moved.

The rain fell fast but didn't muddy the ground. It brought with it a clean smell, although the wet soil beneath her now reeked like compost.

Of death. Decay.

Angie felt moments of blackness and quiet as the sun traced its arc through the sky. Beneath the blackness there were the whispers.

Rest now. You are with us. We are with you. In you. We have held you since the first seed. We have called to every drop. They are all here, they are all quiet.

Water ran between her fingers as the rose swayed under the pelting raindrops.

Join us beneath everything. It's so quiet here. So calm.

Angie was mouthing the words, her lips moving slow, as if in reverent prayer.

You are open to us now, but we've been calling for so long. Your blood answers.

Angie felt no hunger. The sadness that sat in her chest felt thin and weightless. She had to push her mind harder to find her thoughts. When she felt she was conscious, the whispers that fell from her lips came quicker, more frenzied.

You wanted this. You belong here. The world was wrong. Wrong to you.

All you've done is fail.

The last thought was her own, joining the chorus.

You have nothing to live for. Fucking worthless.

The sun fell farther. The rain ceased and dusk light sharpened Angie's sight.

There, at the moment before the sun left the day behind, Angie *saw* the gully.

She saw everything. Around her, rising from the wet earth, was a collection of branches that weren't branches. Twigs that curled like fingers. Whorls in dead wood, open mouths with their lips curled back in agony, puddled with fresh rainfall.

Others had fallen in the gully. Others surrounded her, still and windtorn, weathered.

Nothing lived here. But so many had died.

You belong here.

Every wooden face the light revealed was trapped in a scream. The shapes told her the truth. She was dead center in a splinter of hell and her arm was feeding the darkness under her.

Oh my God, I can't be here. This can't be where I die. I can't die. I just can't. This isn't even happening. It's just a bad trip and

I'm dreaming.

Be with us. There will be no more pain.

Wake up.

What the fuck am I doing here? How did I get here? What did Cypher do to me?

Oh, shit. I followed Kaya.

Kaya.

Angie found she could close her eyes now. She closed them hard, shut out the sight of twisted branches and dead leaves that were pressing closer to her body. The strange, omnipresent sight she'd possesed was gone.

In her head she pictured Kaya on the day she was born. She saw Kaya's new gray eyes staring back at her, smelled the wonderful, strong smell of new life.

Kaya. My angel.

She will die soon. You can be together and no one will hurt you.

Angie felt the words on her own lips. She could hear her voice speaking of her daughter's death as if it were a blessing, an echo of her old fantasies. She'd always hated herself for those thoughts. She hated the voice now.

No! Kaya's only thirteen. She doesn't need to die. She can still be okay, even without me. Even if I'm gone. She's special. She can figure things out, be happy.

Angie could see no light beyond her closed eyelids. Night had returned to her.

Her breath slowed and she found that letting go could be as simple as not trying to breath. Then the scream came, shrill and high-pitched, like an electric shock.

She was a mother. She knew her child's cries like no other's. She ached at the sound and felt light across her eyes. *Sunrise again?*

She opened her eyes.

Kaya stood ten feet away from her, amidst the dead-wood. This time she was thirteen and wearing a long white t-shirt and nothing else. She stared at her mother, directly into her eyes. The glow from Kaya cast a light across the rose that held Angie to the earth. The rose began to wither. Angie could feel blood rushing back to her extremities.

She reached out for Kaya. Kaya's eyes suddenly became wide and filled with trapped-animal fear. Her eyes remained locked on her mother's as the girl's wavering image began to rise above the surface of the soil, even as purple bruises began to spread across her neck and her face turned deep red.

The bruises became the shape of a man's hands, squeezing tight.

Kaya reached out one soft white hand toward her mother, then disappeared. Her dying image was burnt bright into Angie's retinas.

Angie cried out and the sound carried deep into the hollow morass beyond. Her scream was filled with anger. There was no trace of resignation in the sound.

She felt her heartbeat thumping through her body, every inch of her vital and aching.

The flower had vanished.

She wasn't connected to the ground anymore. She rose from the loose soil and stood, swooning until her blood caught up with her head. A sheen of sweat was cooling on her skin as the forest wind slid over her.

The dead wood in the gully around her began to crack and splinter.

She felt movement across her left foot. Something was scraping at her, trying to dig through her skin. Angie tore her foot away and began to run. The direction didn't matter. Her breath was hot and ragged and reminded her that she was alive. She ran as hard as she could away from the empty place behind her, felt it reaching for her and feared she might at any moment be pressed to the earth again.

She ran until she had to stop. The gully was behind her. The swamp trees were receding and she saw orderly rows of cypress in the distance. She'd find her way back to the farm.

She knew that if she kept moving, she'd hit a road.

She'd find a road and then, somehow, she'd find her way home, away from Cypher, back to Kaya.

Hitchhiking hadn't been easy for years. The last few months of random, nationwide crime and spree-killing had made hitching a short step from impossible. Nobody behind the wheel was willing to roll the dice. The odds on encountering inhumanity were way up.

Angie walked twelve miles out of the woods before a long-haul trucker decided to press his luck. As she stepped up into the diesel-belching rig she expected the standard "ass, grass, or cash" pitch, but the man behind the wheel kept it quiet and courteous.

No questions, thank God, aside from wanting to know where she was headed.

She sat down as slow as she could and said, "South Barker, if you're headed that way."

"Yup, I'm rolling through there."

He said nothing else as they rode through the night. Angie zoned out on the roadway in the headlights, tried to calm herself by listening to the rumble of the engine and the thin flow of air coming in through the driver's window.

Angie noticed the headlights of oncoming cars had a multi-color luster to them. She felt like her vision was floating a foot behind her head, separate and disembodied.

She still felt high.

This trip won't ever end.

She shivered at the thought.

The truck driver caught her shiver, switched on the defrost heat.

Part of her wanted to thank him for the gesture, but speaking felt dangerous. She thought that the voice from the woods might find a way out into the world through her lips.

You can end here.

She shivered again. She put her head against her window and felt the cool sink into her forehead, wondered if she had a fever. She couldn't wait until they got closer to the city and away from the tree-lined interstate. Every couple of miles there were fallen trees close to the roadway.

As they passed a large deadfall, she saw something in the flash of the headlights. A body, naked, missing its head, arms and legs spread wide. With a rose tattoo on its chest.

She turned to face the dash and closed her eyes hard.

Just don't look, Angie, don't look. It's not real. None of this is real. Except for Kaya. Just find Kaya. Wait this thing out. Get clean once and for all.

She brought her knees up to her chest and started shaking. She wanted to stop but couldn't.

The truck driver let her off at the first gas station he could find. She saw nothing but relief in his eyes as he said, "Goodbye, Miss. Take care."

Without money Angie figured she had about zero options. She knew she could score some cash by spending some "quality time" in the men's restroom at any truck stop along the strip, but that could wait until she'd gotten some sleep.

Stranded in South Barker. Trapped in a bad acid trip, starved, and dehydrated.

Morning was approaching. She'd spent a day and a half in the woods. Her body moved only because she willed it to.

Angie entered the womens' restroom at the gas station and rushed for the sink. She turned the cold water knob and then cupped her dirt-brown hands under the tap. She was too thirsty to wash first and started slurping back big handfuls of water. She tasted the soil from her hands in her mouth and felt her gag reflex kick up.

We are in you.

She swallowed hard and began to clean her hands, careful to

avoid her reflection in the mirror. She could picture her eyes deep in the sockets, tired, pathetic, pupils blown wide. Pale blue irises surrounded by burst capillaries.

She knew of one place nearby where she might be able to get some cash.

The Courtyard. Rusky owes big time. But there's no fucking way I'm going there until the sun comes up.

She closed herself into the far bathroom stall and sat on the toilet. She put her arms on the handicap bar and lay her head down.

Angie feared resting, feared the doors that could be opened up in her mind, the things this voice in her head might know about. Thoughts she'd had about herself, about her mother, about her only daughter. Thoughts she was trying so hard to purge from her mind. Monstrous things that had always felt hidden until now. The sick, quiet things that no one should ever know.

Despite her fear, she couldn't keep her eyes open.

Her sleep was shallow and visited by voices that begged her not to wake up.

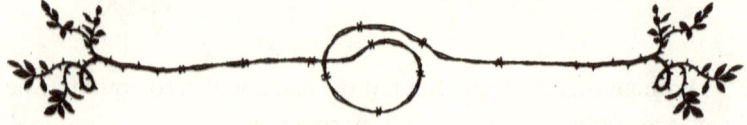

4—Contraction & Expansion

Colleen had called Curtis at 8:45 PM to ask him to come fix her leaky sink. When he arrived with his toolbox in hand, Kaya answered the door. She looked him in the eye briefly and gave him a shy smile—the first she had ever given him—then headed out the door as he entered.

Suddenly he was unaccountably irritated. He felt he should be elated at this break-through with Kaya. Instead he was uncomfortable being in the Smith house and wanted to leave, but Colleen appeared in her bathrobe and ushered him into the kitchen.

He spent an hour lying on his back under the sink, trying to fix the leaking drain. He tried tightening the joints of the p-trap but that didn't help. His bad back was killing him as he shifted around trying to get a better grip on the pipe. The leak got worse the more he tightened the joints. The foul water dripped on his face and ran down his neck into his shirt.

Curtis had smelled mildew before, but Colleen's mildew was the worst. It also smelled like there were dead, rotting rodents under the damp, splitting boards beneath him.

Goddamn this woman—why couldn't she take care of this sort of thing before it got to be such a terrible problem?

Colleen stood in front of the sink, her bathrobe tied loosely so he could look up inside if he wanted. He didn't want to. He wanted her to leave. She was blocking his light.

47

"Turn off the water," he growled at her.

Damn—he'd have to take the p-trap out and replace it. The problem with old plumbing like this was that when you disturbed one area by disconnecting a joint, it often caused leaks elsewhere. Once you started with a job like this, you never knew when it was going to end.

The wrench slipped off the pipe joint and he tore his knuckles open against the rusted housing for the garbage disposal. He cried out in pain.

The flow of water from the leak increased.

"I said turn off the water, damn it!"

When the water didn't cease, Curtis struggled to extricate himself from the tight confines of the cabinet. Colleen grabbed him by the legs and pulled. When he finally pulled his head out, Colleen fell on top of him, pressed her mouth against his and inserted her tongue between his lips. Her tongue was dry, like a cat's, and tasted like soured milk.

Curtis threw her off him, scrambled to his feet.

Colleen lay partially under the kitchen table, looking up at him without emotion.

My family is so distant.

"What's wrong with you?" he shouted at her. "Don't you have any pride at all? Look at the way you live, the way you act. There's a young girl living here, depending on you. Don't you want to be a good example to her?"

"So what—you've come into our lives to make things better?" she replied flatly. "You think you're a good role-model? You don't even work. You think you can buy your way into our hearts with presents and good deeds. And I've seen the way you look at Kaya. I know what you're after."

Curtis wanted to haul her up off the floor and beat her to a pulp.

"You want her, not me." Colleen smiled miserably. "That's fine. You take her and do whatever you want as long as you keep it quiet and keep coming around here and helping out—maybe some money every now and then...."

Rage welled up in Curtis until his vision blurred. He struggled to remain aware of his surroundings. He heard his voice, but couldn't make out what it was saying. At times it was raised to shouting pitch, at others it seemed so quiet and calculating; he was frightened to know what was being said. His animal brain was talking and his rational mind could not keep up.

His anger told him he was telling Colleen exactly what he thought of her and what she should do about it.

Her usually bland, expressionless features flashed with emotion: contempt, surprise, fear.

And shame. Deep shame. He could see the ache of it spreading from her heart to her face, flame-red.

Then he was outside, crossing the street and entering his house. He couldn't locate the half pint of bourbon he'd bought for the holidays last year. He found his bed and lay there sweating for over an hour, listening to his heart rate and waiting for it to slow down.

It wouldn't. He threw on an old corduroy jacket and headed out the front door. He needed a drink.

CAUTION - CAUTION - CAUTION - CAUTION - CAUTION -

"Hey, you all right, pal?"

Curtis had been staring at the varnished surface of the bar, trying to breathe steadily and stop shaking. He couldn't ditch the feeling that he should be ashamed of how he treated Colleen. Until the bartender said something, he almost forgot where he was. He responded quickly.

"I'm not your pal." The anger wouldn't let go of him.

The bartender smiled. "Yeah, I know, pal, but that's what I always call people I've never seen around here before. So, *pal*, what can I get you?"

Curtis ordered a whiskey on the rocks. He asked to buy the bottle, but the bartender said it was a little late in the evening to be acting like a cowboy. Curtis felt embarrassed, paid for his drink, and sat down at a circular table at the far corner of the bar.

He thought of Colleen's offer and imagined undressing Kaya. She would be distant, unreachable. That would help, but still he knew he would have trouble with his conscience.

He heard Colleen's voice in his head. "Do whatever you want," she slurred drunkenly.

The fantasy was shattered. *She shouldn't have given permission. I didn't want her permission.*

He picked up the glass with his shaking left hand and began to drink. As his heart began to slow and his throat and chest warmed up, he bent his head and wept into his arms. The bartender and his scattered clientele paid him no mind. Curtis was surrounded and alone. His memories kept him company and slow sips of whiskey kept him from screaming aloud.

He thought about how perfect things had been when he'd first met the Smiths.

Ever since he'd moved into the neighborhood, Curtis had spent a lot of time sitting at the window of his upstairs bedroom watching the occupants of the house across the street. He had decided that whoever was living in that house would become his family. He knew he could have chosen his family from any in the neighborhood, but that wouldn't be fair—no one else got to choose their family.

He'd gotten information about them online and so knew they were the Smiths, Colleen and her thirteen-year-old granddaughter, Kaya. He watched them coming and going in their car, checking the mailbox and so forth, but had not introduced himself.

He didn't want to give them the impression he was up to something. He didn't want to frighten the young girl before he had a chance to win her heart.

They were not particularly interesting. But they were the easiest family for him to watch, and because he had focused on them, he really had no interest in the other neighbors though he could see their houses and activities with a little extra effort.

One could only have a single family after all.

There were long periods when he could not see them, so Curtis moved his computer and desk nearer the window to allow himself to work online while he watched and he'd gotten a better chair—

one that would swivel and lean back—so he'd be more comfortable.

It reminded him of his lonely habit of sitting in the upstairs
window at the Russell foster home and watching the neighborhood
there. He had spent his teenage years in that cold but efficient home,

watching the neighborhood kids—children with families and friends—play in the streets.

The difference was that when he was a kid, he could sit in the open window and look out at the neighborhood without worrying that folks might think he was up to no good. The kids called him names and occasionally threw things at him, but no one questioned his right to sit and watch all he wanted.

When he became an adult, he had learned the painful lesson that folks did not like adults watching them. He had learned to do his watching from behind window glass with a bit of curtain or blind to help hide his presence.

He slowly learned about his new family, the Smiths. Most of the time Colleen looked totally out of it, her hair a mess, makeup blurred and clothes unkempt. At first he figured this must have resulted from the difficulties of raising an adolescent girl.

Though he had not immediately reacted to Kaya, he had slowly become fascinated with the thirteen-year-old. There was a loneliness and sadness about her that he could identify with. Even though she was emotionally immature for her age, Curtis found her pretty in a lean sort of way, and though he wasn't sure if it was possible, he thought she was getting prettier every day. Perhaps he was just getting used to looking at her.

Colleen and Kaya had verbal rows that could be heard even on the street out front. Sometimes these would spill out onto the front lawn, and once the girl crawled out of her bedroom onto the roof while Colleen argued with her from the window. On that occasion an ambulance, a police car and other official-looking vehicles arrived to settle the dispute.

No doubt some nosey neighbor was responsible for that. Some individuals are so intolerant and judgmental, as if they don't have any troubles in their own family. With that attitude, they're lucky to have any family at all.

Curtis knew that everyone had problems. Getting along with

people was difficult—he should know.

Curtis didn't talk to people much, aside from the checker at the grocery store and the lady who issued him his disabilities check. He kept busy taking care of his house, dusting every day and taking care of the landscaping.

Curtis had been mowing his lawn—the first time since moving in late last winter—when Colleen Smith stumbled across the street, her mouth working as though she were shouting, and waving her arms in the air to get his attention. He'd shut off the lawnmower.

"I'm sorry, ma'am," he said. "I couldn't hear you."

Frustrated, she wagged her hands in front of her face as if to remove the unsuccessful attempt to communicate. She was obviously very high. "When you're through with your lawn, would you mind terribly cutting mine?" she asked. Her eyes didn't focus on him. Then without waiting for an answer, she turned around rather ungracefully and retreated back into her house.

Well, that was forward of her, Curtis thought, but he had been looking for a way into the Smiths' lives. He wanted to become intimate with them. Maybe this good deed was the way in, and if he took care of their unkempt lawn he might begin to feel he had a purpose in the new neighborhood. He'd never felt that way at his old place. Any time he'd tried to help out a neighbor there, they acted like they were suspicious of his motives.

Marcie Davis, a woman who had lived across the street from his old place, had been having a hard time. Curtis could tell just by the way she walked, her posture, the dark circles under her eyes. He had tried to get involved and see if he could help her out. He'd toted her groceries into her house for her, tried to give her a little money, offered to fix up her car, but she'd just looked at him funny, like he couldn't possibly *want* to help her. He must be after something else.

Maybe he was, but that wasn't all there was to him.

He'd been persistent and after a while she wouldn't answer the door to him.

Later she was found drowned in the lake.

Curtis hated to think that it might have had something to do with him.

And now you're pushing another family away, you asshole. You ruin everything you touch, everyone you talk to.

He took another slug off of his drink, heard the bartender shout, "Last call!"

Curtis tried to tell himself that it wasn't his fault that people he knew got hurt, that someone had needed to confront Colleen for Kaya's sake, and that Marcie Davis had problems and he'd just been trying to help.

In the old neighborhood, he'd just been renting so it didn't matter as much that Marcie Davis didn't respond to him. But he'd used sixty-thousand of the one-hundred-thousand dollar payout he'd finally received—after a three-year battle with the paper mill for his back injury—to buy this house outright. He was committed to this spot and the family across the street.

Curtis' *new* family had a lot of problems, but he'd tried to love them just the same. Kaya had difficulty coping and experienced anxiety attacks which could leave her hysterical. Colleen tended to rant and it turned out she looked like hell because she was a barbiturate addict. Curtis used their bathroom on a regular basis, and found the medicine cabinet was a full-fledged pharmacy.

The pills were taking a toll on Colleen. She was fifty-six going on eighty, withering away in a cloud of muscle-relaxers and paranoid visions. Curtis hoped he could help her for the sake of the family. His family. Colleen's addiction was making her into something terrible.

But sometimes Colleen could also be very sweet. The day they met, after he'd finished mowing her lawn, she offered to have sex with him. He'd declined that, but accepted the gin and tonic she offered.

She'd ordered pizza, and they'd spent the evening on her sagging couch in her filthy living room, watching TV. Kaya was on the floor in her panties and t-shirt doing her homework. It was all very warm and easy going like he'd always imagined having a family would be. Curtis pretended to watch the cop show—Colleen's favorite—while watching Kaya. She was thin and graceful, full of promise.

Shortly after they finished eating, Colleen went to her bedroom, changed into a robe, and shuffled to the bathroom. He heard the rattling of pill bottles and then Colleen came out of the bathroom, moving as though the air had turned to molasses.

When she sat Indian-style on the couch, Curtis could smell her vagina. He had smelled worse and not wanting to embarrass anyone, he kept it to himself.

His normally quiet exterior was not a problem as Colleen was becoming increasingly stuporous. Kaya was absorbed in her work, her underwear poking out from under her long t-shirt as she lay on her belly writing in a notebook.

Colleen's breasts sagged in and out of her loosely tied bathrobe. After a while she was asleep, sprawled out on her side of the couch with one leg propped up next to his shoulder. Since she was unconscious and wouldn't notice, Curtis took the opportunity to adjust her bathrobe to cover her exposed genitalia.

No, Colleen was not attractive.

But Curtis couldn't keep his eyes off Kaya. She hummed to herself as she concentrated on her homework. She was fastidious and self-contained. Curtis believed he could smell her from across the room, an island of pleasant aroma in the miasma of foul odors that permeated the residence. Eventually she fell asleep on the floor, curled up around a pillow. He got the impression she did that a lot.

With the TV's remote control, he found *his* favorite programs and watched them late into the night. Eventually he let himself out and went home. He used the tools he carried in his wallet to lock the door behind him.

    I'll get to know Kaya a lot better, he had assured himself, *but I'll have to take it slowly. One day, when she's all grown up,*

when she's mature, perhaps good old Uncle Curtis will be the one she'll turn to when she's down.

But I've messed it all up now. I ruined my family tonight.

Curtis gripped his drink white-knuckle tight and set his memories aside.

I'm going to be alone again.

The thought repeated itself in his head as he left the bar and headed home.

I'm going to be alone again.

The thought was the last one he had before falling asleep.

POLICE LINE DO NOT CROSS

Curtis tried to cheer himself up the next morning. He brushed the whiskey flavor out of his mouth and sat down with a cup of coffee. He worked on the Smith family tree and pretended that the previous night's events had never happened.

He had just completed his work when he heard a loud, persistent knock at his front door.

When he opened the door, a policeman was standing on his stoop. A plump, dark-haired woman was standing on the edge of his property beside the road, with her arm around Kaya.

Kaya was restless beneath the woman's embrace, looking around nervously, pulling at her clothing, but she didn't try to escape. Her hands were filthy and curled into tight fists.

Across the street, Curtis could see police cars and there were paramedics loading a gurney onto an emergency vehicle.

"Hello, I'm Officer Burke with the city police," the policeman said. "Kaya Smith says you're her Uncle Curtis."

Curtis would have smiled if he hadn't been so surprised by the situation.

"That's right," he said. "What's going on?"

"There's been an accident. I'm sorry to tell you Colleen Smith is dead. We're still trying to determine what happened."

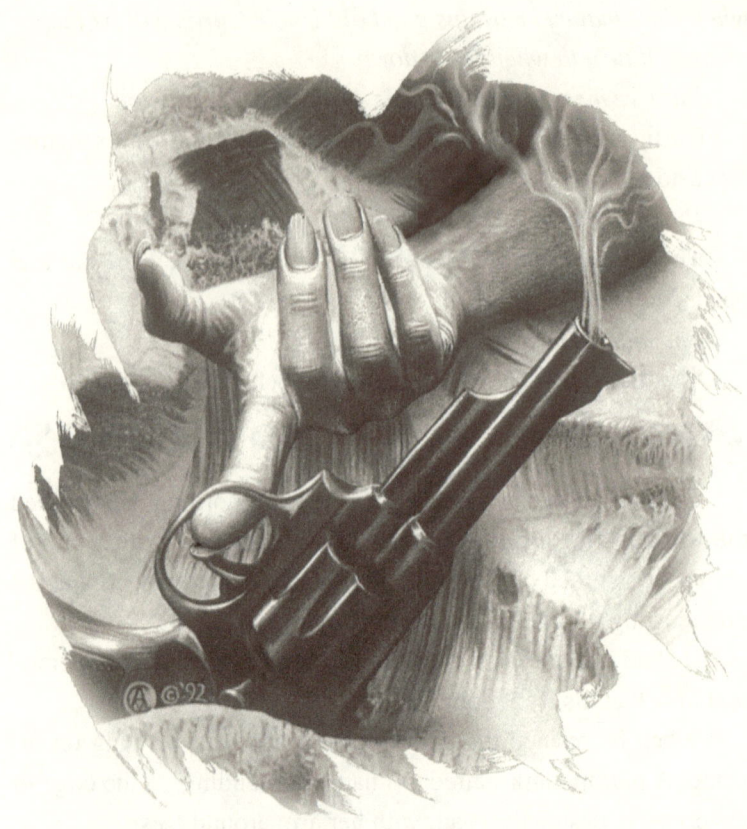

"She shot herself in the head, Curtis," Kaya yelled to him from across his yard.

The policeman leaned in and dropped his voice to a near-whisper, obviously annoyed at the girls interruption. "We don't know that what the girl says is true. An investigation is still pending."

I did this, Curtis thought. *I have destroyed my new family. I've lost them.* He looked at Kaya standing beside the road with the woman. When she glanced in his direction, he saw no evidence that she might blame him.

No, I haven't lost them entirely, he decided with some relief.

"We're in the process of trying to locate Kaya's mother, and Kaya says you're the only family in the area. Is this true?"

The lie came easily. Inside his head, Curtis had been a part of her family for quite some time.

"Yes, I'm her Uncle Curtis. I mean, I'm not technically her uncle. I'm her third cousin, once removed on her mother's side, but I'm blood. I mean, that's what matters, right? And I've been like a father to her."

Officer Burke looked at him for a while before saying anything else. His eyes held Curtis steadily and were filled with suspicion.

Curtis decided immediately that the less said, the better, but then something occurred to him and more words spilled from his mouth. "I've been working on a family tree. It shows what I'm talking about. It's on my desk. Would you like me to get it and show it to you?"

"No, sir. That won't be necessary. We do want her to be with some kind of family right now, but first we've got to take her to St. Matthew's Hospital and make sure she's okay. Can I see your driver's license?"

Curtis said, "Why?" and knew immediately that he was messing up whatever chance he had to hold onto his family. The cop was going to peg him as a liar if he didn't calm down. "I mean, of course. I'm sorry, officer, I'm just in a bit of a daze right now. This is so unexpected. I mean, I know Colleen had some problems, but…"

"Sir, can I see your driver's license? Please don't make me ask again."

Curtis pulled it from his wallet and passed it to the cop, focusing all his will on his hand, trying to hold back the shakes. Officer Burke wrote down the information.

"All right, Mr. Loew. Can you tell me where you were around 12:45AM this morning?"

"Yes. I was at that bar with the red doors on the corner of Turner and Cadillo."

"And what's the name of the bar, Mr. Loew?"

"I don't know." He had no idea what the place was called. He had walked into the first bar that had a neon OPEN sign in the window. "But the bartender will remember me."

"Okay. Listen, we've got to get Kaya to the hospital and get her taken care of. She's filthy and looks like she might have jaundice and malnutrition, and she's in quite a bit of shock. Please stay at your residence as much as you can today. I'm sure that after we talk to Kaya we'll have some additional questions to ask you. So don't go anywhere, all right Mr. Loew? It's in your best interest to stay put."

Officer Burke looked into Curtis' eyes for a moment longer, then turned and walked toward Kaya.

Kaya began to yell. "Curtis! Curtis! No, don't let them take me. I'll be all alone. You have to come with us." There were tears welling up in her eyes. "I won't go unless you go!" She struggled against the woman's hands, but she was small and held tight.

"Please, Uncle Curtis!"

He looked to the cops with pleading eyes. Officer Burke stepped back toward Curtis.

"Mr. Loew, I've decided I'd like to keep a closer eye on you until we know exactly what is going on. You can come with us, but if you speak to Kaya it must be done clearly and loudly, agreed? You can console her verbally but we don't want anyone putting any ideas in her head until we get a chance to ask her some questions."

"Of course, officer."

"All right, Mr. Loew. Let's go."

Kaya had no obvious injuries, so they took her to the hospital in the patrol car with an ambulance driving point. Curtis and Officer Burke sat in the front seat. Kaya and the woman, a child welfare worker named Martinez, sat in the back. Miss Martinez tried to give Kaya a teddy bear. Kaya refused it.

Curtis looked back through the grating at Kaya.

"There were leaves in Grandma's mouth, Curtis," she said. "I pulled them out so she could breathe. Why were there leaves in her mouth?"

Curtis shook his head.

Officer Burke turned to Curtis. "We took them from Kaya and bagged them as evidence, but found no indication that they came out of Mrs. Smith's mouth."

Kaya insisted. "She was full up, Curtis. With leaves."

5—Plans & Pavement

Angie awoke in the bathroom, starving. She used sopping wet, brown paper towels to clean the excess mud, dirt, and blood from her skin while her stomach grumbled and cinched up on itself.

She looked in the mirror long enough to register she wouldn't pass for normal until she ditched her threads, regardless of her bathroom sink cleansing techniques.

Her dreams had been filled with bad whispers and dark and twisting shapes like pink slugs writhing over each other in the darkness. Insects with too many legs tore the flesh from the slugs and oozed black blood from their mandibles.

She'd slept without comfort for what she'd thought was a brief moment, but as she walked out of the bathroom she was confronted by sunshine, nuclear-bright in her still-blasted pupils. She squinted and her stomach grumbled again, a persistent engine rumble she couldn't shake.

Shit. I slept for hours and nobody disturbed me. Cleaning the bathroom must not be top priority.

She wanted to laugh at the thought. She wanted to pretend that she was just on a bender and, boy, wouldn't people think her "waking up in a public restroom" story was a laugh and a half. The unshakable acid-waver tinge to the air in front of her and the specter of her daughter in pain kept her somber and driven.

She stole a bottle of water and a Rice Krispie Treat from the gas station. If the clerk with the gin blossoms and backwards cap

noticed, he didn't bother to stop her. She didn't care if she was profiting from apathy or charity. She was famished.

She walked along the interstate, heading south out of South Barker, hoping her short skirt and jutting thumb could hook a quick, quiet ride to nearby Pennington.

If Rusky's still at The Courtyard, he's got Cypher's money. As long as he doesn't know what happened to Cypher, I can cop his cash and split.

She pictured herself running game on Rusky. He had a soft spot for her. He'd be a pushover.

Shit, Rusky, just give me the money. Cypher was nice enough to let you in on this deal and I'm sure that's the nicest cut you ever made off some boosted valium. So, if you don't want to hurt my feelings and make Cypher mad, you better kick over Cyph's share.

Rusky wouldn't want to make Cypher mad. Fuck, nobody did.

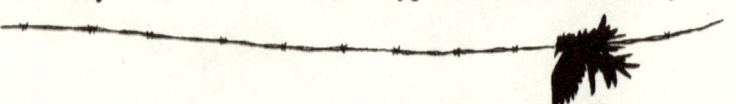

Another truck, another uncomfortable trucker. This driver was nice enough to pick Angie up and take her to the outskirts of Pennington, a mile from The Courtyard. He wasn't nice enough to talk to her.

She had even wanted to speak to him, for just a moment, to hear the sound of someone else's voice, maybe to clean the sounds from the forest out of her skull. She was going to ask the driver what his name was. It was a simple question. As her lips began to form the words, she'd felt a terrible pain in her head, like icicles jammed through her eyes. Then that *voice* came tearing from her mouth.

YOU ARE ONE OF US ONE OF US QUIET CALM HE IS OTHER HE WILL KILL YOU HATE YOU SLEEP CALM QUIET QUIET.

The soft, pleading whispers of the forest had left her, replaced by this shriek that shot her head through with noise and sent a trickle of blood dripping from her right nostril.

She had pressed her palms up against her eyes until the pain subsided and discreetly wiped her bloody upper lip on her shirt.

Angie had felt the sounds coming from her mouth, but the trucker hadn't reacted. It was as if her voice had become a frequency too strange for him to hear.

She didn't try to speak to him again. She was afraid the voice would return even louder, that the vessels in her brain would vibrate with the sound until they burst. So she rode in silence. Quiet and alone.

The nameless trucker sounded scared and relieved as he said goodbye.

Angie knew that something was wrong with her. The bad vibes from her hitchhike chauffeurs just confirmed that other people could sense it. Despite her inability to ask the trucker's name, he'd never offered it to her.

It wasn't bad trip paranoia. If she were just high those truckers would have been all over her, dropping conversation, innuendos, questions, observations. Truckers were starved for that shit.

No, something *wrong* had tainted her. People knew it, and felt it. She was giving off cancer vibes, repulsion.

We are in you. Always. Every last one of you will sleep.

It was her lips that wrapped around the words and spit them out, but never her voice that sounded.

Shut up! Goddamnit, get the fuck out of me!

She felt the whispers inside her hush again. Anger seemed to keep the voices at bay.

Listen to yourself, Angie. Rationalizing your shattered mental status by pinning your trip on some weird shit you saw in the woods. Look, there's no rose on your arm now, and there never was. Your fingertips aren't made of twigs. The forest isn't after you. The voice you keep hearing, that's your own brain's bullshit, but the volume's jacked way up by some bad fry. Get your shit together. Focus on getting sane, getting home.

She found these thoughts strangely comforting, but she couldn't shake the sound of the other voice out of her head. It was low and hungry.

Angie shivered and looked toward The Courtyard.

The Courtyard was a mile away. It was the wrong place to be, but she couldn't think of any other source of cash flow. She picked up a jagged rock and began walking in the direction of the old cement buildings that made up The Courtyard.

If one of these crazies tries to touch me, I'll crack his fucking skull wide open.

Angie hated The Courtyard.

It hadn't been a proper jail for over eighty years. The iron bars had long since been salvaged, the tile removed or shattered, the windows broken. All that remained at the bottom of the yellow grass valley was a conglomerate of cement buildings with a central courtyard that housed an empty fountain.

The fountain had once held a stylized statue of Justice and her scales. All that remained now was a graffiti-riddled stone torso. Last time Angie and Cypher had been down here to visit Rusky, someone had placed the bloody head of a pit bull on top of the statue.

The place was often host to brutal dogfights. Three months ago Cypher had made her watch two Rotts scrap it out while she was on some heavy mushrooms. She found the whole experience terrifying. It wasn't what the dogs did to each other. It was the faces of the men surrounding the hounds.

Reptiles. Cold eyes on every last one of them.

As Angie walked closer to the buildings, dry grass crunching underfoot, she couldn't help but wish Cypher was with her. The Courtyard was no place for women.

Men were at their lowest here. Half of them were crazy, psych ward unwanteds ejected from the asylum by state budget cuts. The other half were worse. They knew what they were doing and just didn't care.

She hoped she could find Rusky, make her case for the cash, and bail fast.

Angie looked to her right and saw a starling, dead and dried to a husk, hanging from a strand of old rusted barbed-wire. The breeze rustled his feathers and made his body shift on the wire. His out-stretched claws reached to the sky as if he were merely trapped.

Angie could identify with that.

The closer she got to the buildings, the more human the air smelled. Booze, urine, shit. The three most common smells at any human gathering place. Crickets buzzed and flitted away from her footfalls. The sun was approaching its zenith.

She stepped into The Courtyard as quietly as she could. The place looked dormant.

Hangovers must have pushed the bum cancer into a brief remission.

She almost laughed at the thought, but she caught a quick motion out of the left corner of her eye. A black shape moving fast across the entrance to the building marked "F Block."

Angie gripped the rock in her hand tighter.

Jesus, what am I doing here? If I'd just bowed out on Stacy's invite to the rave, I'd still have my sanity. I'd probably be in a nice rental car right now, window down, breeze in my hair, headed back to see Kaya with a working head on my shoulders.

I hope Cypher is dead.

She remembered where Rusky was squatting last time she and Cypher had visited.

"A Block." She had thought the label was hilarious. The cement box was indeed "a block."

She scanned the area. There was "A Block," two buildings past the old fountain, on the right. She moved toward the building as fast as her thrashed platform shoes would carry her, tucking her black hair back over her ears to keep her peripheral vision open for Courtyard residents.

She heard movement everywhere now and pushed faster, running into "A Block." As she entered, she felt the temperature drop and the smells of human decay became thicker. She remembered Rusky's cell/room was on the left, toward the back. Her footfalls echoed against the gray cement as she ran. She considered yelling out Rusky's name just so he'd know she was here, in case one of his fellow tenants tried to pull her into a room.

She heard *his* voice first. Three cells ahead on the left.

"OhmyGodohmyGod…oh sweet Lord, oh don't let it crawl deeper…."

She stood at the entrance to his cell and the smell of sickness hit her.

Rusky was curled up in the corner, wearing a yellowed white t-shirt and a pair of dark green shorts. His shoulders were barely wrapped in a thin black blanket. His eyes were wide and fixed on a finger-wide gash in the top of his thigh. He was prodding the wound with a fork, insistently pressing down like it wasn't his flesh.

"God please, don't let it in...."

The blood that ran from the wound on each side was already dark, coagulated. He'd been at this for some time.

Angie spoke. "Hey, Rusky."

She felt the voice, *that* voice waiting behind her lips, a dull presence behind her eyes, as if it had become aware that she was speaking to another human being. She felt it, but this time it did not bring sharp, icy pain. This time it wasn't screaming at her. It whispered again, soft and insistent.

Two are meeting two are one and will pull each other into....

She tried to push the voice out of her head and stay focused.

"Hey, Rusky!"

He didn't turn toward the sound or seem to register her presence.

Prove to me I'm real.

Angie had zero patience. "Hey, Rusky, you fucking meth-head tweeker!" She threw the rock in her hand at the opposite corner of the cell. It crashed and shattered. Rusky jumped and turned to her, pupils pinpointed as sunlight came in through the foot square win-dow to his right.

"Angie. Angie. Angie." He said her name like a mantra and it seemed to calm him.

"Angie, the centipede got in last night. Now I can't find him. I don't need any more legs. I DON'T NEED ANY MORE LEGS." He shouted at the hole in his leg, making sure the centipede got the point.

Angie reeled, her stomach hitched. She hadn't seen Rusky this bad before and didn't know how she was going to get her cash.

Angie decided to play it maternal. She wanted the cash more than she wanted to comfort Rusky, but he'd been kind to her once, when no one else had been.

A little over a year ago Cypher had started doping her up and inviting his friends to trade drugs and business favors for a free fuck when she was at her least coherent. She dug the dilaudid skin pops and most times she barely remembered the fumblings and prodding of Cypher's cronies. He kept her so high that she didn't eat much, so by the time Rusky had gotten around to buying a piece of the action with a bottle of Grey Goose, she was malnutritioned and her skin was turning yellow. Rusky had entered her room and turned the lights on. Even through the haze she could see his face go slack. He had flinched and turned the light off.

He still fucked her, but afterwards he made Cypher drop her off in front of St. Peters Hospital. She got re-hydrated off of intravenous and the state health plan picked up the bill. Three days later she walked back through the front door of Cypher's house. Cypher and Rusky were sitting on the couch, chopping rails on a vanity mirror. Cypher looked up at her, smiling.

"I told you, Rusky. You train a bitch right and she always comes home."

Rusky had laughed, dropped his head, and snowplowed a fat yellow crank piner.

He saved my life, for whatever that's worth. Now I have to talk him down off this insect trip and get my money.

The vision of her daughter reaching out for her, neck blooming with black handprints, re-entered her mind as she walked toward Rusky. Angie crouched down next to him and watched his hands, wary of having the fork he carried jammed into her chest.

"Hey, Rusky, what are you doing?"

"Trying to catch him."

"The centipede?"

"Yeah. He goes deep right as I poke down and then he comes back and looks at me when I close my eyes. I can't see him, but I can feel him looking, you know, like when you're driving in a car and you start to stare at somebody and right away they turn their head because they can feel it, you know, just *feel it*—that you were looking at them." Rusky turned his head and stared straight and deep into her eyes, begging her to understand, to really know what he was talking about. She played along.

"Yeah, I totally know what you're talking about. That happens all the time. Even when I'm walking, like on the street or whatever, I can feel it when people look at me from cars." The smell from Rusky's wound wafted up into Angie's face. He was ripe. She tried not to gag.

"I can help you get him out, Rusky."

"NO, you can't. *You* fucking can't. He only knows what's in *my* heart, that's why he came for me in the first place. He wants to live in my heart, to take it over. He tells me that he's inside me. He says he always has been, inside, you know, but I felt him crawl in by my hip last night."

Angie's mind flashed on her nightmare, the creature with too many legs tearing pink tissue and spitting up black blood.

She shook the image from her head and tried to think of some way to calm him, to change the topic, but it was clear that Rusky's mind was Centipede Central and wouldn't take other thought traffic for quite a while. She knew meth visions didn't shake easy and kept working the motherly instinct.

"Hey, Rusky, did you ever think that maybe the centipede doesn't want to hurt you? That maybe he'd make your heart feel good if you let him in?"

"That's what he says, that's what he says! He says he can make things quiet for me. But there's something wrong about the way he says it. He sounds like Cypher sounds when he wants something."

She knew what he meant. She knew why he was afraid. And she knew Rusky's fear could be used as leverage.

"It's kind of funny you say that, Rusky, because Cypher does want something." She leaned in closer, watching the fork in his hand. "He wants his share of the money from those blues you moved last week. He needs it today. That's what he sent me for."

Rusky's eyes sharpened, meth-head paranoia mixing with real fear in his face.

"Angie, no, no, no. No, no, no."

"'No' what, Rusky?"

"No. You're lying to me. Cypher already sent someone for that money."

"What?"

"Yeah, he sent that Irish kid, O'Rourke. The Irish guy's the one that tried to rob me. He wanted all my money, not just Cypher's.

He's the one that pinned me down and dropped the fire into my eyes, out of his little breath mint dropper. That's when the centipede got into the room, right after O'Rourke left."

She'd heard about O'Rourke forcing bad acid on people before, but all the assholes Cypher hung out with told stories like that. And most of the time, according to Cypher, they were just stories. Guys trying to one-up each other on the psychopathic street cred.

But O'Rourke had fried Rusky's brain. No story. Just this mess, this real, rotting mess in front of her. Angie felt like she was floating behind her head now. This was just *too* wrong, and even as she watched Rusky gouge deeper with the tines of the fork, the MONEY stayed at the forefront of her brain, squashing out the soft whispers that tried to tie her tongue.

In every one of you every one of you in the other all drifting down....

She pushed it out of her head, although the pain behind her eyes had returned.

"Rusky, do you have any money left? Did O'Rourke get everything?"

"Maybe."

"Maybe what, Rusky? Either he got it all or he didn't."

"He's going deeper, Angie. I... can... feeeel... him... crawling."

Angie gave up on words. Her brain went simple.

She grabbed the fork from Rusky's hand and then moved it to his throat so quickly she shocked herself, but held it steady. She saw his jugular bulge beneath the crusty metal tines. His eyes were on hers, wide with disbelief.

"Do you have any fucking money?"

"Angie, what are you doing? What the hell are you doing?"

"Rusky, if you have any money, I need it now." She looked into his eyes.

He read her eyes, caught the life or death gravity of the situation. "Yeah, I've got a plan."

"I don't need a plan, Rusky, I need some fucking cash."

"No, no, no. *A plan*, Angie, a plan where I hid the money. I wanted to keep more than my share and I heard Cypher's hurt real bad so I thought I could get away with it. When O'Rourke started hitting me, I told him about the plan but it was too late. His blood was up. His eyes went bad and he wouldn't listen. But you listen to me, huh, Angie?"

She nodded.

"Yeah, you listen, and you know about the centipede. I can show you my plan, but you have to move that fork away from me and let me stand up."

She did it, stepping back and checking behind her for any Court-yard residents who might have been aroused by the yelling. It ap-peared that nobody really cared. She figured screams were com-monplace in these halls.

Rusky stood slowly and shifted most of his weight to his good leg, going light on the muscle he'd dug a trench into. He reached behind his back, into his shorts. Angie heard the elastic of his un-derwear rasp against his skin. She watched as his face grew red and the veins on his neck bulged out. He grunted, and then his face relaxed.

He pulled his hand out of his shorts. A small, oblong piece of metal was in his left palm, offered up to her.

"It's my plan, Angie. I keep it in a secret place. Now you and me and the centipede are the only ones that know about it."

He twisted it in his hand and it unscrewed at its midpoint like a big metal gel-cap. She could see the twenties and hundreds he'd pilfered crammed inside.

. Angie reached forward, holding the fork in front of her, and tried to pull the bills from the stinking metal without touching its edges. Rusky grabbed his plan tighter, and the money was suddenly in her hands. She peeled off a one hundred dollar note, dropped it for Rusky and put the rest in her pocket.

Rusky started laughing. "Go ahead and take it, Angie. I know where I can get more now."

"Where's that, Rusky?"

"Oh, the centipede says I shouldn't tell. But... I don't know. Maybe I didn't tell you that Cypher doesn't like you anymore. And maybe I didn't tell you that he'll pay me if I tell him I saw you. Shit, I bet I even know where you're headed. There are whispers in me now, when his legs move, and he tells me things, secrets to me, on the way to my heart, with him. Homeward bound when he doesn't stare. The centipede knows things. He knows you, he says. He's waiting for you to sleep."

Angie felt like stabbing him in the throat with his fork, but she had the money and she remembered the time when Rusky had been kind.

"Rusky, please don't tell Cypher anything. Will you promise? Please promise on everything that you won't tell him." She pleaded with her eyes, tried to find that good spot that he had in him, somewhere.

"I don't know, Angie."

Angie was about to tell him that he was a good person, that he could do the right thing and keep her secret. Instead she felt the voice at her lips again.

QUIET TOGETHER EACH VOICE FALLS NONE MEETS QUIET ONLY US HERE TOGETHER ALWAYS ALONE THERE UNTIL YOU FALL QUIET.

Her head filled with pain, like molten steel poured in through her ears. She became dizzy and swooned but remained upright, aware of the tenuous balance of power in the cell. She looked to Rusky, figuring he'd be even more confused by her uncontrolled outburst.

"Did you hear that, Rusky?"

"Hear what, Angie? I mean, I saw you whispering to yourself but I...."

"Wait, my lips were moving but you didn't hear a sound?" She could not wrap her brain around what was happening, couldn't make the pieces fit and function.

"I don't know, Angie, I just don't know. I'm scared. I'm so scared."

Angie was scared, too. She tried to calm herself and looked into Rusky's eyes.

"It's going to be okay, Rusky. Everything's going to be okay."

The lie, like all the others before it, came easy. She turned to leave. She pretended that she didn't hear Rusky say, "I'm going to be okay," as she walked away.

She hit the sunlight and the open Courtyard air with Cypher's drug money in the tiny pocket at the front of her skirt and Rusky's bloody fork in her right hand.

Shapes moved in the buildings around her, but nobody came after her. She hoped they were just scared of the fork. She realized that they probably didn't mess with her because they'd seen her here before—with Cypher.

He's waiting for you to sleep.

Cypher, the centipede, the woods. They were all waiting for her to sleep.

The burnt-retina image of her daughter reaching out for her kept her awake.

She dialed in an anonymous 911 call at the first pay phone she hit. She could swear the woman on the other end of the line giggled when Angie said, "There's a man at The Courtyard that needs medical help right away."

It was the best she could do for Rusky. Maybe some med-tech would be stupid or ethical enough to brave The Courtyard and get Rusky the hell out of there, detox him and keep him safe in a clean, white hospital.

Maybe.

Or maybe the voice on the other end of the phone would still be laughing when she hung up, and Rusky would be alone, trapped in an open cell, being watched by tiny eyes beneath his skin.

Angie spent one hundred and twenty dollars of her ill-gotten half grand. Seventy bucks went to the bus ticket. One way on the 4:30pm shame train to Monahan, home to Colleen and Kaya Smith. She hoped they'd be there at least. It had been so long....

Twenty bucks went to a pair of thick gray sweatpants and a hooded sweatshirt to match it. One dollar bought her a pair of thin white cotton panties. She had slid them on slowly and found the feeling of the fabric comforting. She'd been open and hurting for too long.

Five dollars bought her a used tan military backpack with "Perry Harver, 7th Grade, Mrs. Horning Homeclass" written across the top in black felt-tip pen. The remaining twenty-four bucks filled her backpack with junk food, soda and water, and bought her a walkman with tiny bud earphones. She'd ridden the bus before. She knew the best way to make it through the long hours was with music.

The bus station was half-filled before her departure. A short, stocky man with two tattooed tears by his right eye scoped her body out, his look long and slow, despite her dumpy gray outfit. The man's eyes on her body made her think of Rusky's centipede, always watching.

Cold filled her belly. She gripped Rusky's fork, which she had placed in her left pocket. There was something comforting and warm about the metal.

The smell of rotten milk breezed through the bus station, thick in the hot, humid air. The smell reminded her of Rusky's excavated leg.

I wonder what Rusky is digging with now. Poor fucker.

Her fingers wrapped tight around the fork, ready to strike if Mr. Tattooed Tears wanted to get to know her any better. Holding the fork felt ludicrous, but safe. It was the first safe feeling she'd had since she'd left Stacy's.

I don't have to worry about this fucking guy. He can stare at me all he likes. I just walked into The Courtyard, robbed an acid casualty with a fork, and walked out without a scratch. So what if this guy killed two people? Shit, the tattoos are probably fake. He's a commodities broker slumming his day away at the bus station with press-on tats, looking for intimidation kicks to keep him hard for his little domestic wifey at home.

Still, if he sits by me on the bus he's catching this fork in his fucking eye.

Angie kept her anger at high-tide. It focused her and forced the voices and the ugly LSD edge out of her brain. She could hear her teeth squeaking against each other as she ground them together. Her adrenal glands were dumping hard, flushing her system, priming her paranoia. It felt good.

It felt lonely. She was angry, untouchable, and detached from the world. Even the bus station flotsam kept their eyes to the linoleum when they walked by her.

She sat down at the end of a row of blue plastic chairs and hung her head, hoping the voices from the woods had finally left her. A cold feeling in her snack-saturated belly said they were wait-ing.

This is bullshit. If I had some fucking reds I could just pop, pop, fizz, fizz, and float the bus trip away. Things would be quiet. Things would be nice.

Her pulse doubled. The dope dream sounded too much like echoes of the voices that wanted her to sleep, and be calm, and let go. She remembered the figures in the woods, their gnarled wood fingers reaching up from the earth, their faces supplicant to the sky, stretched in agony.

I don't even know if Kaya is still alive. If what I saw has al-ready happened....

At 4:27PM she boarded the bus in a cold sweat.

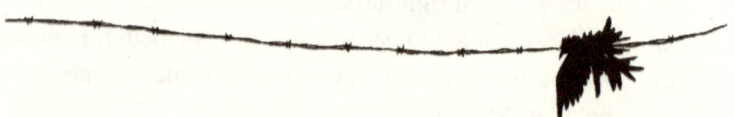

Travel time on the shame train. Ugly, slow time on a bus that wheezed and clanked its way to Monahan. No companion in the seat next to her.

Animals can smell disease.

Angie felt surrounded. The bus was near packed, and breath-ing other people's old air upped her claustrophobic leanings.

Despite the density of people around her, she felt loneliness at the forefront of her chest, a dull pounding that didn't fade with time.

I'm surrounded by people that would cross a busy street blind-folded to avoid bumping into me.

She hadn't felt like this before. She'd never felt so separate from the people around her.

Too much time around Cypher. Too much time away from the world.

She wondered what would happen if she closed her eyes and kept them shut. Could she just disappear? Who would notice?

Cypher would. She had his money. She had set his balls on fire.

If I just disappeared, he wouldn't get the pleasure of killing me.

The idea was appealing in the worst kind of way. A way that rang true and told her it was dangerous to think too much until she could screw her head back on. She gazed out the window.

Tan crop fields and beige strip malls with garish neon signs passed by, a homogenized blur of commerce and pavement.

There weren't enough distractions to shut out her thoughts and memories, to keep the whispers away. She put on her walkman and cursed herself for not buying any tapes. She rolled the tuning dial to the clearest station she could pick up and tried to zone on the voices that floated in through the static.

The hours and miles passed. Angie tried to keep her brain active and angry, to push down the cold fire that sat at the base of her stomach. She forced herself to remember unwanted memories, and listen intently to the voices she could discern amidst the white noise on the radio.

"...which marks the fourteenth time this year that we've seen this kind of senseless murder in Ellis county. Officials are still unsure what has led to this rash of public shootings, and no general profile for the shooters has been compiled. Anne Pushman, 34, of Clover's Dell shot seven people, including her own children, at a Dari Rite market last August. (static) ...asked why she had done it she replied, 'Attention must be paid.' Attention must be paid, people. (static) ...yeah, Jim, I do think that's from *Death of a Salesman*. Do you think the crazy bitch owes some royalties? (laughter....)"

I'm eight years old. I won't eat my peanut butter and honey sandwich because the honey tastes gross and has made the bread all soggy and squelchy. Mom puts out an egg timer in front of my plate. The ticking is fast. It makes me nervous. Mom sits across the table from me and stares. She just stares, almost like her eyes are going right through me, and her lids are heavy and she's breathing loud and slow and I've been watching her swallow big black pills all morning. She says they are vitamins. They make her weird. My time on the clock runs out, the bell rings, and mom snaps back into her eyes. Her face remains calm as she grabs my arm and pulls me out of my chair. I hit the floor hard but I don't have time to cry out because she's yelling, my mom—Colleen, you fucking doped up old bitch—is yelling at me.

"Can't you see them? They are dying, and you won't eat your sandwich. Give him your goddamn sandwich so he doesn't die. You don't deserve it. You should be hungry."

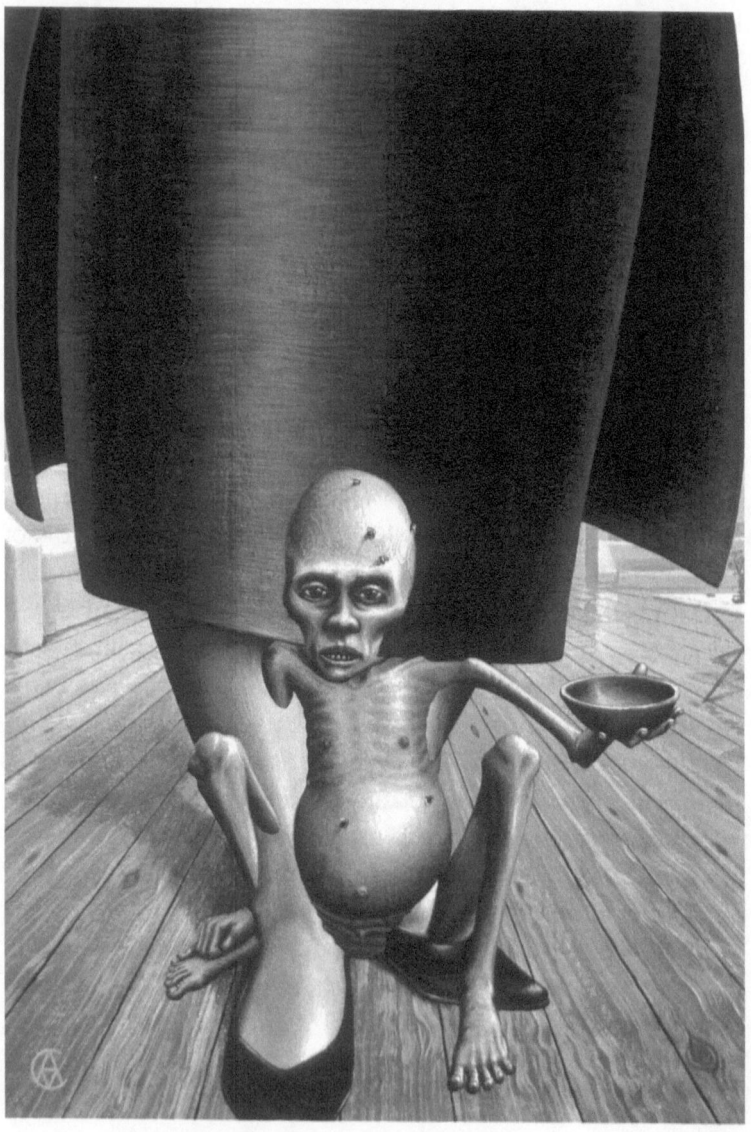

There is no one in the room except for me and mom. She turns away, pulls my sandwich from the plate, and throws it to the kitchen floor.

It sits there for weeks.

"...his wife, Margaret Ashbaum, reports that he had been acting distant before he made the decision to stop speaking and eating. She says that he had spoken... (static) ...and she thinks his recent unemployment may have been a factor. She has no explanation for his decision to lie naked in the garden behind his house. Medical officials and county health say that if he doesn't return to the house soon and begin eating, they will forcefully...."

I am sixteen. I am alone in a subway bathroom stall, and the floor beneath me is wet and spotted with blood.

Peter said he wanted to be there for the birth. That was until he realized the kid wasn't his. Couldn't be. He'd used a condom that one time and had been too drunk to even come. And he'd been hearing stories about me, true stories I couldn't pin a doubt on. I'd been wanting someone, anyone, to take me away from my mother and give me love. I'd found only words in those other boys, but Peter's love had felt real. Peter was on the football team. Peter had good grades. Peter would run his fingers through my hair when I was sleepy. He was my chance for escape, my chance for real love, and I blew it by sleeping around.

He'd asked me for the truth. I had been desperate for him, but not enough to lie—he'd been too kind. But once he knew the baby wasn't his, we never shared another word. Nobody was there for the birth. Nobody gave a shit until the transit cop found me. He said I was white as a ghost. I just couldn't stop bleeding. I held Kaya in my arms, against my chest, for as long as I could.

I'm sleeping on the street with Kaya wrapped in my coat when the police pick me up. They tell me I can't have her out on the street like that. The state says I'm an unfit mother. They give her to Colleen.

"...new projections indicate that over 70% of the population will have experienced some form of identity theft within the next three years...."

I'm eighteen and Colleen tells me it's about time I start taking care of Kaya. I come home. I spend a week at mom's hanging out, cleaning up after the dirty old bitch. I sleep in the same bed with Kaya and watch her chest rise and fall in the mornings. She is perfect and calm and her skin smells so clean and good, and I hold my hand above her mouth and feel her warm breath roll against my skin. I hold my hand up against my mouth and try to breathe in whatever is inside of her that makes her so perfect, so peaceful.

After seven days with Kaya, she starts to trust me and smile at me.

After seven days I can't breathe.

I'm no mother. It's better that Kaya never know me. She needs so much. She only smiles as long as I keep giving.

I don't even leave a note when I bail. I kiss Kaya on the forehead, walk out the door, drive into the city, and buy a handful of percocets.

I dream for days. I cry when I'm sober.

"...Iran will continue to press for development of a nuclear arsenal despite protestations of nearly all...."

I'm twenty four. I've been on a two-month ecstasy binge and can barely speak without sobbing, the serotonin drought is so bad.

I tell Cypher I've been thinking about killing myself. I tell him I've hit rock bottom.

He says, "Dig in and get comfortable."

He hands me another Mitsubishi pill and asks me if I can do him a favor.

"...committee says that with the opening of the Kinshasa Highway to increased traffic, the rate of AIDS infection could cause levels of mortality unseen since the bubonic plague... (static) ...spite the best efforts of educational programs, the rumors of a 'virgin cure' persist. Those seen as pure, particularly the young, and often even infants, continue to be the victims of rape, and in some regions...."

I'm twenty-eight. Cypher thinks I'm asleep on his ratty, green couch. He is talking to Brody Kirkenhaur.

"The secret to making sure it doesn't happen again, to really

let them know you mean business, you know, that you are class A
un-fuck-witable, is to get their family. So with Pearson, we put his
kid and his girlfriend into trash cans out front of his house. Not all
of them, I mean, we dumped a lot of shit, and buried some of it, just
to lay up the odds, but we made sure that when him and his neigh-
bors went to throw away the trash they'd catch an eyeful. I mean,
can you imagine that shit? Fucking dude picks up the lid to throw
away some old Chinese food or some shit, and bam, there's his
fucking little boy's head staring at him, like, 'Daddy, why?'"

Cypher and Kirkenhaur bust a gut. I pretend I'm in dilaudid
heaven, barely breathing.

I try to tell myself that Cypher wouldn't really do anything like
that. I revise history and imagine Cypher was just on some tweeked-
out fever rant. After all, the guy's not exactly Honest Fucking Abe,
right?

Still after hearing what he said, I'm haunted. Every time I see
spilled trash, the shit is half human. Ring fingers hanging out from

under trashcan lids, like worms crawling free....

Almost a year later I'm lucky enough to listen in on another
conversation. This time Cypher and O'Rourke are talking in a ho-

tel bedroom while I swoon away the end of a whiskey and nitrous bender, holding onto the edge of a toilet in the dark. Their voices are hushed but urgent, almost joyous. I think I can feel the vibration of their voices through the porcelain I'm clinging to.

"Jesus, O'Rourke, I can't believe how easy it really—"

"You call that easy. Bullshit, man, the old lady almost caught you with her knife."

"Yeah, old mama bear was definitely defending her cubs. But she didn't get me, and besides that part, it was easy. Not physically, I mean, but doing it, really doing it. Getting in there. I looked them each in the eyes. At first it was too much, I had to look away, but then the feeling of power just...."

"Yeah, it was good. I can see why this shit's on the rise."

"Yeah, O'Rourke, it was so good. Worth doing again. There's something to it... something I can't figure out... I don't know...."

"Hey, Cyph?"

"Yeah?"

"You're zoning, dog. Let's get cleaned up."

Cypher steps into the bathroom and flips on the light. My head spins as I turn it, but I can still clearly make out two dark red drops of blood on the front of Cypher's shell-toe sneakers. I begin to dry heave, but it doesn't last. My heart's beating too fast, my eyes go static, and I pass out.

I up my pill intake and try to sleep as much as possible.

But there's no sleep, no rest to be found. The lies I used to tell myself have become recognizable as bullshit even through the Vicodin haze. I never really believed Cypher loved me, but I'd felt a sort of safety... the safety of important property, owned and desired. There was a feeling that my life had value to him.

Those two deep red drops of someone's blood were quivering, liquid proof that the lives of others had no value to Cypher. There was never any love or devotion to shield me.

I could be dead at his whim. Killed for kicks. They say the one that kills you is usually someone you know. And at that point I finally feel I know Cypher, really know what he is.

And I'm not ready to die. But what do I have to live for? What I am now, what I've become, this half-blind lab bunny sucking cock for painkillers? This isn't a life.

I have to restart. I have to go back to square one and build a new life over the old. I have to make things right. That means getting away from Cypher, getting home, getting back to Kaya. The younger me. The pure me. A second chance at love, at everything.

So one night while he's out of the house, I leave him. It feels like a death sentence, just as much as staying with him did, but now there's a chance. It's like the governor could call. I could be free somehow.

But a month later he found me, and poisoned me.

I hope he's still burning.

The sun had long ago set outside Angie's window. Her eyes were closed and her head rested against the glass. Her breathing was short and tight, racing to keep up with her heartbeat while she relived the nightmares inside her head and fought sleep and sadness like they were death.

She was thinking of the woods, of Kaya's hands reaching out for her. She thought of how she used to wish, in her lowest moments, that Kaya had never been born. Now Kaya's existence was all that kept Angie breathing, and she was afraid that upon seeing her daughter again those dark wishes would return to her. She wondered if she could ever truly be a mother to the girl.

Angie'd forgotten she was even on a bus until it slowed and lurched to a stop, the squealing brakes audible over the fuzzy radio voices calmly feeding fear and alienation through Angie's headphones.

The bus doors opened, allowing a rush of warm wet air into the stuffy vehicle.

The sign to Angie's right said "Monahan's Finest Bus Station." The digital clock next to it read 5:30AM.

She waited until the bus was empty, gathered her things, and stepped out onto the sidewalk. She turned toward the rising sun and began to walk to her mom's old house.

Two blocks from the bus station she felt her belly tighten up and the hair on her arms prickle. Her lips moved against each other. Something stole her voice and spoke.

Come home to us. We are waiting for you.

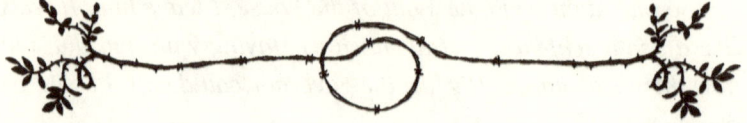

6—The Decision to Bury

After Kaya's physical exam at St. Matthews, she was taken to a hospital room. She cried out for Curtis just as she had on the street between their houses. Her outburst could be heard even in the waiting room. Curtis was both proud that she was demonstrating to everyone how much she wanted and needed him, and embarrassed that everyone would think he'd raised a child that was a pain in the ass. He thought he saw the woman at the nurse's station give him a cold look. A disgusted Officer Burke came for him and escorted him to her room.

A tall, middle-aged physician who couldn't make eye contact with anyone in the room, explained that despite being undernourished, Kaya was in fairly good health. "But she's pretty traumatized," he said. "She should stay the night just for observation." Then he left the room.

"Tomorrow," Officer Burke said, "Kaya will go stay in a shelter until her mother can be found."

Kaya said quietly and matter-of-factly, "I'll run away again."

Curtis could see the edges of hysteria in her nervous eyes. He looked to Miss Martinez.

She took a deep breath, let it out slowly, then looked at Officer Burke. "I've had this case for a long time. Her situation's been minimally adequate and she's had some problems staying put. Took us nearly a week to find her last time she ran away."

Officer Burke nodded his head. "Tell you what, Mr. Loew, I'm gonna check you for prior arrests and any outstanding warrants. If you're clean we'll consider letting her stay at your place for now."

He walked away.

My juvenile record should be sealed, but what if he has a way to get at that information? Curtis broke out in a sweat despite the cool hospital climate.

For just a moment he could smell gasoline and smoke and hear the cracking of boards that had preceded the collapse of Murphy Hall, the foster home where he had stayed when he was twelve.

There had been so many eyes on him after that, none of them with any kind of love in them. Just scorn, fear, and blame. He felt as if he had walked through a bad vapor that day, something that he carried with him that kept people at a distance.

Technically any information regarding the fire should have been expunged. But if the people at the courthouse lied to him, if those documents still followed him....

"Curtis, excuse me?"

Curtis snapped out of his mental drift and tried to pretend he'd been paying attention to Miss Martinez. He furrowed his brow to show interest. He'd seen people do that before and hoped it read true.

"Do you have a room in your house that could be prepared for her," Miss Martinez asked, "so she could have her own bed?"

She's trying to tell me not to sleep with her. Curtis felt angry and guilty at the same time. He remembered his decision to say as little as possible to these people. They could read him if he reacted. He responded in a calm monotone.

"Yes, I could fix her up with her own room."

"Your house would have to be clean, you understand. We would have to check it out."

"Yes." Curtis knew they would find his place to be spotless.

"Kaya, Curtis needs to go home now and you need to rest. Curtis, we'll let you know whether or not she can come home with you tomorrow."

"No," Kaya whined. "I'll run—"

Curtis cut her off. "I'll be back tomorrow to take you home with me. You get some sleep, Kaya." He was proud of himself for being firm with her and pleased when she didn't challenge his authority.

He left the room and the hospital, but returned an hour later to drop off Kaya's pillow. It was the one she curled around when she slept. Before he entered the hospital, he pressed it to his face and inhaled as deeply as he could. The smell, so delicate and human, made his heart race.

There was a different woman at the nurse's station when he dropped off the pillow. She took it from him and offered Curtis a slight smile.

As he left the hospital and headed home, he thought about that smile, what it indicated the nurse might have thought about him. Curtis always had difficulty seeing himself. He tended to take his cues from others.

The woman probably thought it was sweet of him to bring Kaya her pillow. She probably thought he was Kaya's father.

Curtis knew that Kaya wouldn't have been comfortable without her pillow. Bringing it to her seemed like a natural thing to do for his daughter, or cousin, or whatever. He knew what it was like to sleep in a strange bed. It could be difficult. That someone saw what he'd done as a thoughtful thing—the sort of thing a father might do—made Curtis realize that he *was* being thoughtful and that others were capable of assuming that this was natural and good.

I am her special person now. I can make her happy. But... those fantasies and dreams....

His face flushed. The fantasies he had involving Kaya would have to go. He would have to banish them. She was family.

From now on he would be a stone man, impervious to the strawberry smell of Kaya's hair, the newfound sway of her hips. She would be able to sit in his lap, hug him, express affection in all the ways a daughter might need to do with her father, and he would be

able to return that affection without feeling hot, and sick, and excited.

Curtis hoped it would be as easy as making the decision to change his attitude, but feared it would not.

He'd just have to make the effort, and if he failed from time to time, he'd have to keep trying. As long as he didn't make Kaya uncomfortable, he figured he'd be doing okay.

Now if the police didn't dig too deeply into his life, then everything might turn out just fine.

For him.

For Kaya.

For what they were becoming together.

CAUTION - CAUTION - CAUTION - CAUTION - CAUTION -

Curtis was allowed to take Kaya home the next day. Miss Martinez explained that he was expected to make her life as normal as possible and make sure she got to and from school. She also gave him a schedule of when she would be checking in on Kaya.

Curtis wanted to get across the street and do a little painting in Colleen's bedroom—there were stains on the wall beside her bed that shouldn't be seen anymore. *And while the paint dries, I can watch some of our old home movies.* But Miss Martinez had told him that the police would not allow anyone over there for a minimum of three days while they processed the scene. He just needed to keep Kaya from going over there until he could get the painting done.

Curtis found it difficult to wait that long. But on the morning of the fourth day, after taking Kaya to school and after he'd seen Officer Burke come and rip down all the yellow crime scene tape, he couldn't get to Colleen's house fast enough. His hands were shaking with excitement as he opened the front door to his family's house.

7—Dawn Over Monahan

A sheen of sweat coated Angie's skin, but it didn't cool her. Instead it felt hot and sick and stuck to her like the early morning's humidity.

She walked quickly through her old home town, trying not to reminisce as she passed the old shop fronts and garage-sized bars that littered the suburban sprawl.

She couldn't help but stop for a moment in front of Radeker's Pharmacy. She saw someone moving around inside. *The boss is at work awfully early this morning,* she thought.

A glance through the window confirmed that little had changed. The same collection of greeting cards, useless trinkets, beauty aids, and medicine littered the shelves, showing little semblance of organization.

Not that Clancy Radeker needed to keep the place tidy to turn a dollar. He made a decent load of cash milking old ladies for their Social Security and offering deals on pills that weren't necessarily prescribed. Colleen had often sent Angie here on errands, always asking her to pick up a couple of little things on top of her dope. Angie had bought bubble gum and Christmas ornaments and tiny porcelain dolls that cracked too easy. It was her first experience in drug dealing and she dug the kickbacks.

Seeing a new SUV the size of a small elephant parked beside the pharmacy, she smiled.

There's my fucking college money. Thanks, Colleen.

She spit on the hood of the rig and kept walking.

A few cars passed her as the muggy morning crept toward dawn, but nobody slowed down or recognized her. As she rounded the corner of Marker Way and Pierce Street she heard two cats screeching at each other in someone's backyard. She knew how the heat could do that to animals. People, too. The heat made them crazy. It clicked over a little switch in people's brains so that it was now possible for them to do that wrong thing they'd just *thought about* before.

The dawn felt ugly, filled with animal tension. She let it into her system, breathed hot air in hard and exhaled with a shaky breath. She clenched her fists. Sweat rolled down the cleft of her lower back. She threw an ugly look at a passing hatchback, causing its passenger to rapidly avert his gaze.

Anything that keeps the voices down is fine by me. Even if I have to be angry for the rest of my life.

Angie passed a bar with red doors and a glowing neon OPEN sign in the window. The old neighborhood layout was clearer to her than ever. She was two blocks from home.

Home. Jesus, is that what it is?

Her pace slowed. She smelled burned eggs and decayed lawn cuttings. The cats had ceased their yowling.

This was never my home. I don't belong here.

Angie remembered the looks the neighbors used to give her when she would play in the permanently yellowed front yard. They looked at her with disgust; they *aimed* it toward her as if she could help the way she lived, as if she had wanted to wear a dirty blue jumper every day, as if she had wanted her hair to be matted, as if she were the reason her mom lay around the house all day popping pills and leering back at them.

Colleen, in her finer moments, used to call the neighbors Purity Pollys and Church Club Cunts. Colleen said, "Let them lose a husband, you know, just let them lose a husband. Then they'll know." She used to grin at the sentiment as if she just couldn't wait for the next widow to be made.

Maybe she could invite the neighborhood women over for gin and nembutols! What a social club that would make!

One block's distance from her old house, Angie found she could barely step forward. Even the thought of Kaya, hands outstretched for help, didn't move her. She'd been running for so long, and now, just moments from the concrete front porch of her childhood home, she stopped.

The sun was coming up and the pink-orange streetlights overhead were clicking off. Moths still flocked to the bulbs. Angie could hear their soft bodies bumping into the lights above her, a muffled percussion. Angie could see her house in the glow of the morning sun.

What the hell *am I doing here? What am I going to do, walk in and tell them the truth?*

"Oh, hey, Colleen. Hey, Kaya. A couple of days ago I was drugged and raped by a sociopath, and then I almost got sucked into the soil by some evil trees in the middle of the fucking forest. Anyway, after all that I got this weird feeling... okay, it was a vision, really, and I thought maybe Kaya was in some kind of trouble so I hitched my way out of the woods, robbed an old acquaintance with a fork, caught a bus, and decided to drop by. Oh, and I've been talking to myself, saying all kinds of weird shit, but it's not really my voice so please just ignore that if you could. So how've you guys been?"

Angie laughed at last and though nothing felt real enough, she felt like maybe she was moving toward something good. Maybe she could just drop in and be with her family again and make things be all right. It was the first time she'd felt this way since she'd purified her blood and mind in the tiny room at Stacy's house. She thought of Kaya's delicate feet wrapped in pink ballet slippers, both of them dancing together, spinning.

Angie smiled.

She began walking again.

Yeah, maybe things will be okay. An unexpected sense of relief washed through her, the first clean feeling her body had known since Stacy's.

The relief was quickly washed away by the pain that hit her chest as she crossed the street toward Colleen's house. She felt warmth spreading from the sharp pain on the surface of her skin.

You are never alone. Never hidden. We are in you. We are waiting. We need you.

Angie unzipped her hooded sweatshirt and saw the blood

spreading from the tattoo on her chest. Standing there on the sidewalk, she was confronted by the knowledge that nothing, absolutely nothing, was right.

Her lips moved.

Come home.

She turned her head toward the roof of Colleen's house. The light coming from the rising sun blurred in her peripheral vision, took on a rainbow hue. Ice spread through her belly. She felt thorns at her chest. She heard skin and fabric tearing in unison.

No. This can't... I just let the anger go for a second... I mean....

She hunched over on the sidewalk, trying to remain standing, although the slight weight of her backpack almost toppled her.

Colleen's house stood to her left. Shapes moved to her right. A big black Labrador knocked over a trash can.

She turned toward the sound and saw half of a child spilled in the street, sprawled on its back in pieces amidst the empty bottles, greasy fast food bags and old newspaper. The child turned over

onto its belly and tried to crawl toward her, one arm made from a bent shipping tube, the other made from glass, paper and some sort of shellfish.

Angie turned her head away.

This isn't real. This can't be real. It's just the acid, still just the acid.

She turned toward the house and tried to become angry, tried to close her eyes and beat the visions out of her head and think (*just think*) like she *had* been doing.

The pain in her chest was spreading.

No!

She turned her head upward, refusing to look down at the blooming stain on the front of her shirt.

None of this is real! I don't want to see it anymore.

Come to us. Walk. Behind the house. The woods. Things will be better there. There are already so many of us there.

She refused to move, refused to listen to the oily-voiced urgings coming from her own mouth. She took a step toward Colleen's house with her head upturned.

That was when she saw the dead body on the roof.

Oh God, Kaya used to sneak up there to hide and play with her toys.

Her eyes were transfixed on the body. It was too young to be Kaya, too small and worn away. It was in pieces, rotten. Its head turned toward her, knotted eye sockets regarding her without emotion. Its tiny mouth opened wide and black oil began to run from its throat, trickling down the roof. A starling landed on its head, paused for a moment watching Angie with its one empty, beady eye, and then tore at the roof-thing's body with its beak. A high pitched whine came from the thing's throat as the last of its oil was vomited across the eaves. The whine crescendoed and began to tremble. The sound became Kaya's voice in a long and unshaken squeal.

Angie heard the shuffle of trash across the street, the other shape crawling toward her. The thick reek of old milk and discarded fat floated into her nose and mouth as it crawled closer.

She felt needles across her arm and envisioned the rose thorns weaving their way down to her wrist.

The Kaya-scream of the baby-shaped thing on the roof grew louder. She turned back to the half-child on the street. It feebly lifted its glass and paper arm and reached out in her direction with its rotting-crab-hand.

Angie found the strength to run. She did not move toward the back of the house, knowing in her belly that if she were any closer to the woods she wouldn't be able to stop her legs from heading deeper into the thicket beyond.

Angie ran up to the front porch, opened the front door, slid inside the house, and then slammed it behind her and locked it.

The bleating of the creature on the roof died as if a gust of wind had blown it to nothing. She risked peeking out of the glass arch at the top of the door. She expected to see the garbage creature staring back at her with its rotten eyes seeping rancid milk, but it was gone. The black lab was rooting snout-deep in an empty bag of Oreos. The trash around the dog was only trash.

Angie looked down at her shirt. It wasn't clean, but the spreading crimson pattern over her tattoo had disappeared.

Relief washed over her, heavy and fast.

She breathed deep, taking in the new silence, and letting her eyes adjust to the darkness inside the house.

Then she yelled out, "Hello, is anybody home?"

There was no answer, only the sound of something shifting rapidly in the den at the back of the house.

If nobody's home, then why was the front door unlocked?

A noise again, from the den. Whatever had shifted was now settling.

Angie dropped her backpack to the floor. She took a step forward and felt something plastic crinkle under her shoe. She reached down and picked up the balled yellow plastic. She smoothed it and read it by the dim glow of the streetlamp coming in through the window's arch. In between the tattered edges it read "INE—DO NOT CROS."

Her belly went ice cold again, and looking down the black hallway toward the den, she contemplated turning around and facing the faded acid visions she'd left behind.

Or maybe I should just head out to the woods and sleep. Things are so wrong.

Another sound came from the back of the hallway. Like a playing card inserted in bicycle spokes, a plastic sort of ticking.

Angie pulled Rusky's fork from her sweatpants pocket and walked down the hall. Adrenaline flushed through her system. Her spit dried up, leaving her mouth metallic. She reached out and opened the door to the den.

A man sat half-naked in the cramped den, resting on an old green loveseat, wearing only a pair of blue jeans. He had shoulder length hair and deep set eyes that were fixed on the wall opposite him, where an eight millimeter projector was casting Colleen's old home movies onto a sheet tacked to the wall.

On the makeshift screen, Angie was five and playing with a plastic doll. Her lips moved but there were no words, just the constant flip-flip-flip of the film and the steady breathing of the stranger in her den.

His head turned toward her, and he regarded her with fear and surprise in his eyes as if there was no way he ever expected to see another living being at this moment in time.

He opened his mouth.

"Hi, um… I'm Uncle Curtis. Oh, God, um… I'm *supposed* to

be here. I've just been painting.... Are you a neighbor or with the police or something?"

Angie felt her legs turning soft. She wavered and had to focus just to stay upright.

"Who the fuck are you?" She held the fork out. "I don't have any fucking uncles. None that will talk to my Mom. And why the hell would the police need to be here?" What she wanted to ask was, *Where's Kaya?* But she couldn't tell what this guy was up to, and if he was part of a home invasion she didn't want him to know Kaya even existed.

She realized this guy could be a friend of Cypher's or some twisted fuck who Cyph hired to take out her family. Had he already gotten to Kaya? Was this the man whose hands she'd seen bruised into the flesh of Kaya's neck?

The man calling himself Uncle Curtis stood slowly, putting one hand to his back and grunting as he rose. He stayed across the room, wary of the fork. Angie noted the fear in his eyes, strange for a man hired to kill her.

On the screen Little Angie was talking to herself in a mirror. The camera shot jiggled a bit. The operator must have thought Angie was funny.

The man spoke again, stepping slowly toward her. "Colleen's your mom? You're Angie, Kaya's mom?"

Shit, he knows about Kaya. "Yeah, and who the fuck are you? Stop moving right now, Goddamnit, and tell me who you are."

"Well... it's weird, but... listen, I don't know how to explain this to you right now and you look real upset and I can understand that, but I'm not here to hurt you. I'm Kaya's uncle, Uncle Curtis, and I...."

"Shut up! What the hell are you talking about? You're not my uncle, my brother, my anything. I don't know you. Our family doesn't know you so you shut the hell up. Where's Colleen?"

Angie watched the man's eyes and saw a real sadness come into them. She couldn't tell if he was acting or not.

"She's dead. I'm sorry."

Angie snapped.

This isn't right. This man killed her. He killed mom and Kaya, and now he's going to kill me.

Angie swung forward, jabbing Rusky's fork into the man's face just above his right cheekbone. The man hit the floor and blood welled up from the four punctures and began dripping from his face to the dark green carpet.

Angie felt a sudden and heavy pressure in her gut as the man rocked up from his position on the floor and threw his left shoulder into her abdomen. The weight of his body pushed her all the way out of the room and she hit the hall wall hard enough to leave a circular dent where her head cracked the wall.

She felt plaster tinkling down onto the part in her hair and tried to steady her vision. She regained sight long enough to see the man calling himself Uncle Curtis run from the den and out the front door.

Angie wasn't sure if he was coming back, but she could barely move and felt the throb at the back of her skull grow more insistent.

Maybe... he's coming... back. Hide. Hide.

She slumped forward on the old shag carpet and crawled toward her old bedroom at the beginning of the hall.

I can get in there. I can lock it. Curl up, hide, be quiet.

She stopped for a moment, feeling the heavy pressure just above her neck and the carpet rubbing her knees as she dragged them behind her.

My mom's dead.

She pushed into the her room, which was currently furnished with only an old mattress covered wrinkled black sheets.

Angie reached up to lock the door behind her. She could barely focus to reach for the knob, but after pawing it for a moment and pausing to feel a dry heave rise from her gut, she managed to lock it.

Safe. Hide.

My mom's dead.

Angie could barely even hear her own voice as it spoke.

She is with us now, all the voices are one. Join us. You can rest here.

Angie's clothes were twisted tight around her from crawling across the floor. She felt as if they were growing tighter by the second, as if the fabric was shrinking against her skin and trying to reduce her. She struggled to breathe and managed to strip down to her underwear before collapsing into the mattress.

She pulled the thin, black sheet over herself and curled up in a fetal ball on the mildewed mattress. Unconsciousness took her and she slept in blackness. Her chest barely moved, pulling shallow breaths from the air of her childhood home.

8—Rest & Motion

She had tried to put his eye out!

She was probably trying to kill him. She was dangerous, a wild animal, Curtis told himself, and—if he had a gun—he'd be within his rights to hunt her down and shoot her.

He had watched the Smith house on and off since returning to the refuge of his own. He didn't want her to sneak up on him. As far as he could tell, the woman claiming to be Kaya's mother had not left the place, unless she'd done it while he was in the bathroom get-ting a Band-Aid for the four seeping puncture wounds beneath his eye.

As he became calmer, he wondered just how dangerous she really was. He winced at the pain below his eye. No telling where that fork had been. He knew from conversations with Colleen that Angie lived on the street a lot, that she was an addict, and that she didn't give a shit about the welfare of her daughter.

He was scared of her, scared of what she might do to him and what she might do to get Kaya away from him. She obviously knew something about fighting, the way she had attacked him and got in the first blow. Or was that just the conditioning she'd had out on the street?

Curtis wanted to pack Kaya into his car and leave town, but then the police would be after him. Then he thought to call the police and tell them that a known drug offender who had no claim to Kaya had broken into Colleen Smith's home and attacked him, but he knew he didn't want to draw that much attention to himself.

101

Damn!—he was stuck here looking out the window to make sure he knew what the crazy woman was doing. No telling what she'd do next. He didn't want to lose track of her. Maybe he should get a kitchen knife and go over there and... what? Kill Angie? Threaten her? Offer to buy her some drugs if she'd go away? Buy her enough drugs to cause an overdose? Was any of that really possible?

He had to do something—Kaya would be awake soon, and he'd have to help her get ready and take her to school.

He worked up the courage to go back to the Smith house and look around. He took a butcher knife from his kitchen with him, tucked in his sleeve. Shaking a bit as he hurried across the street, Curtis hoped if anyone were watching, especially Angie, that they wouldn't notice the sharp angle of the blade beneath his shirt.

He felt like such a chicken shit. He wanted to run, but knew that if he didn't take care of this now, the situation might catch up to him later when he and Kaya were settled, happy and least expecting it.

The door was still open a crack. Inside the house was silent. He found the locked door off the hall and carefully opened it using one of the tools from his wallet. Angie was inside, passed out, ly-ing on her right side on the old mildewed mattress.

Curtis stared at her for a while as his pulse rate slowed. There was something wrong with her. Her breathing was ir-regular. Saliva had drooled down her chin and dried there. She didn't have the peaceful look of someone sleeping. Curtis had the im-pression that her brain wasn't functioning properly. It gave him the creeps. She obviously was no danger to him now.

What a waste of adrenaline. The sudden let down left him feel-ing twitchy and indignant. He wanted to bash her head in. How dare this bitch attack him!

He leaned over and put his knife to her neck. Should he just slit her throat and be done with her? He could wrap her in a tarp, haul her off into the woods beyond the house and bury her. No one would be the wiser. It would be hard on his bad back, but he could do it. Certainly no one would miss her.

Curtis wasn't feeling as tough as his thoughts suggested. He knew the consequences of committing crimes and how persistent the police could be in tracking down a perpetrator.

He spoke into Angie's ear, "Wake up."

The woman mumbled, and her feet, sticking out from under the bed sheet, shook a little. He put aside the knife and shook her by the shoulder, calling out her name, but this didn't rouse her either. He shook her harder and turned her onto her back.

Perhaps she was overdosing without his help.

How lucky can you get?

No, Curtis couldn't stomach that attitude and he pushed the thought away. This woman was a human being and, he admitted reluctantly, a family member, but she was the one who had abandoned her family so he didn't owe her much help.

Wanting to keep a low profile, taking her to the hospital was out of the question. He decided to monitor her condition in his spare time. That was all he would do. With a little rest, she'd probably come out of it and be fine.

When she got sober, she might not be so dangerous.

He rolled Angie back onto her side.

If she died that wouldn't be such a terrible thing.

Curtis sensed that he had some time on his hands before Angie's tormented body made a decision to either let go or return to the land of the living.

He had to get Kaya off to school. He'd had her home from the hospital for just two days and knew that any deviation from her regular schedule would draw unwanted attention. He decided to take Kaya to school a little early and then spend some time on the internet digging deeper into Angie's family history.

I need to know who and what I'm dealing with.

He turned the bedroom light off and said, "Why'd you have to come back?"

There was no response, only the slow, shuddering sound of Angie's breathing.

Kaya was awake when he returned. She moved through the house like a ghost, silently brushing her teeth, using the toilet without flushing it, then going into the kitchen to pour a bowl of cereal and eat it. The one time she glanced up at him, she seemed to notice his injured eye, but said nothing about it, for which he was grateful.

Kaya was never willing to speak just after she got up. He had learned not to bother talking to her until she had been awake for at least an hour. So much the better this morning. What he had on his mind was not something he wanted to tell her about. No, Kaya didn't need to know that her psycho mother had returned and was passed out, probably overdosing, just across the street.

Perhaps if Angie died he could dispose of her body and then Kaya would never have to find out about her.

He drove the girl to school in a car filled with heavy silence.

POLICE ▮ ᴺᴱ DO NOT CROSS

After taking Kaya to school, Curtis looked in on Angie three times. The first time he discovered she had pissed and shit herself. There was a pool of thin, watery vomit by her head, matted into her hair. Disgusted, he'd left her and gone back to his house and his computer.

He continued his exploration of the Smith family on the genealogy web sites he had been frequenting. His intention was to look back in time, to find the dirt on Angie. He found several personal genealogy pages that were filled with text from tombstones, last wills, diaries, court and police records. He'd follow a lead until it ended, backtrack, pick up another, and follow that. There were a lot of dead ends, but as long as he was willing to backtrack and pick up a new trail, the information seemed limitless. Much of it was pretty dry reading, but occasionally he ran across something juicy.

And it all belonged to him now. He'd always wanted to have not only a sense of family, but of history, of being a part of the world around him, a feeling that his existence had made some kind of dent in the seamless passage of time. Curtis copied and pasted into a word processing file everything he could find on the Smiths and then printed it.

He found more dirt in the Smith family than he had anticipated. There was a high frequency of insanity and there were a lot of unusual deaths and murders. There were a lot of holes in the record he was assembling, the edges of the holes suggesting deep, dark secrets.

In a journal compiled by an Andrew Smith of McMurto, Virginia, the author joked about the family being the product of a "gunny sack of bad seed." He recounted, for example, the miserable life of Lily Winthrop, a well-known New York City prostitute and thief.

Lily Winthrop, born 1840, died 1873, was born in the notorious Old Brewery at Five Points in New York City and never saw the light of day until the place was razed to the ground by the City and the Missionary Society in 1852. It is said that the Old Brewery, which had been a tenement since 1837, housing up to one thousand people at any given time, was the den of every imaginable criminal activity. Murder was perhaps more common in this dwelling than any other in the world at any moment in history. When it was cleared out for its destruction and to make way for a new mission house, the police rounded up dozens of wanted men and women as they fled the dilapidated structure. Workmen carried out of the place over a hundred sacks filled with human bones taken from inside the walls, floors and cellars.

Lily Winthrop was also carried out, malnourished and squinting at the light of day. She was immediately adopted by a family belonging to the Missionary Society, but she appreciated none of the new life offered to her. She was but an animal with no morals and no conscience. The family let her go and she returned to the Five Points and lived the rest of her life on the street, a thief and prostitute, having neither friendship nor loyalty toward anyone. She gained notoriety and a place in history by being such a nuisance and liability, even in the rough Five Points area, that she was universally hated. On her 33rd birthday she was murdered. Her dead body was found in an alley, disemboweled and nearly decapitated. Her murderer was never caught. Apparently not much effort was made to find the killer. Because she was so thoroughly hated by everyone in the area, Lily's corpse was left to be eaten by rats, cats, and dogs. It took only a day and a half for her bones to be scattered.

"It's all genetics and learned behavior," Curtis heard himself mouthing absently. "They pass it on one generation to another. It makes sense that Angie and Colleen are related to this woman."

But Kaya's different, right? She's special. She won't turn bad like her mom and her grandmother.

She's got me now. We'll protect each other from the world, and won't let it turn us rotten. We'll protect each other with love.

As Curtis read several other accounts in the journal of wretched Smith lives, he became more and more uncomfortable with the idea of being a part of the family. Even so, the relief he felt considering the fact that he wasn't truly a member nagged at him.

No, I don't get to bow out just because I'm a little spooked. Every family has its troubles; mine is no different.

He pretended the nagging was merely his conscience, encouraging him to do something about the mess Angie had made of herself. As long as he put that energy back into the family, the lie was something he could live with.

Curtis gathered up a bucket, a clean wash rag and towel, and walked across the street.

He used some old paper towels of Colleen's to sop up Angie's vomit and strip it from her matted hair. He was surprised to find himself sniffing the paper towels, and was even more surprised they didn't reek of alcohol. Curtis rolled Angie onto her back and pulled the sheet off of her. Holding his breath to avoid the stink, he tried not to look at her crotch as he pulled her panties off. He was surprised to see that they appeared to be brand new. He took the panties to the bathroom to clean them and put some warm water in the bucket. Returning to Angie, he started cleaning her crotch with the dampened washrag. He wiped out the cleft of her buttocks and then her thighs. He tried not to look too closely at her vagina, but soon found himself cleaning it, exploring its folds.

For someone who had spent so much time abusing herself, Angie was still rather attractive, he thought.

He wondered if he should stick his finger inside her to make sure she was clean in there as well. Then he noticed how hard he had become, how tight his swollen skin felt against the rough fabric of his jeans. Cleaning her had put a fire in his belly, and he realized he could open her legs a little wider and put himself inside her if he wanted to....

But she's family. She's one of us.

No, as much as he wanted to be close to her, to feel her newly cleaned skin against his, it wasn't the right thing to do, not with a member of his own family.

He closed his eyes and imagined himself to be the stone man, but this time he was burning with desire. The flames were licking him all over and he had to do something quick to stop it. He imagined the flame changing color, from hot orange to warm yellow to cool green and finally icy blue.

Curtis shivered with the cold thought. His erection had gone away.

He got a blanket out of the closet and rolled Angie up in it.

He took the bed sheet to the bathroom, washed it and Angie's panties out in the sink, then returned to his house to take a nap.

Although he'd slept very little since the day Colleen killed herself, he found he couldn't rest. His heartbeat was trapped in his ears, loud and repetitive. He closed his eyes and found only the shallowest slumber.

CAUTION - CAUTION - CAUTION - CAUTION - CAUTION -

The third time Curtis checked in on Angie, he just sat and watched her sleep for about half an hour then left to go pick up Kaya.

He shut the bedroom door behind him, and was walking toward the front door when he heard the sound. It was a low sound, muffled by the pressed wood of the door, and couldn't have been Angie's voice. There was a depth to it that prickled the hair on Curtis' arms and filled his belly with ice.

He turned back, reached for the doorknob and heard the sound again. He couldn't quite make it out, but it sounded like an old man whisper-ing, "Let go."

Curtis threw the door open, unsure of who the hell had crept into the room without him noticing.

There was only Angie barely breathing, face empty of emotion.

He could swear he'd heard the voice though. It had been almost desperate sounding.

Let go.

I need more sleep, Curtis thought.

He closed the door again and left to pick up Kaya.

Family, after all, means responsibility.

9—River's Crossing

Angie's condition was closer to coma than sleep. She slipped from brief moments of near-conscious panic—*Oh my God, who was that man? Where is Kaya? What's happening to her? Why can't I move?*—to long periods of darkness.

The darkness was punctuated by yellow light, a sickly dusk-light forcing its way into her mind, opening it to visions she could not look away from.

She saw Kaya, gasping, lying supine on a kitchen table beneath "Uncle Curtis." His thick, rough hands were wrapped tight around her delicate throat. A high-pitched whine tore from Kaya's mouth as she whispered her last breath. The sound was followed by thick gouts of black oil bubbling from her lips, seeping from the corners of her bulging eyes. "Uncle Curtis" wept above Kaya's body while the black oil dripped from the wooden edge of the kitchen table and watered a bed of creeping, tar-black, thorny vines that slithered over each other like sharp snakes seeking out the last of her daughter.

The terror of the moment brought her briefly from her unconscious vision, and though she couldn't open her eyes, she could feel her real body for a second. She could feel hot vomit rolling up from her guts and soaking the rough old mattress. She knew her bowels were letting loose, but there was no feeling of shame, or even nausea, only a release of intense pressure. She knew her skull was pounding and that the room now smelled like a mixture of shit and old soil, like the ground she had been tethered to in the forest.

"I'm still alive," she thought, but her return to consciousness was brief and shallow. Dusk-light filled her mind again. She found herself at the edge of a river, staring at the cool water as it drifted by. She wanted to jump in and let the water rush over her and fill up her ears so she could hear the sound of her heart. Across the river, beside the tall, eroded bank, something was moving, although the movement was slight enough to have been almost nothing.

Then she saw the shape. He, or it, was half submerged in the swiftly moving water. The shape rested; the broken branches that formed its ribs seemed to rise and fall as the water flowed by. If it had a mouth, it did not need to move it to speak to Angie. The voice was inside of her head.

It's so perfect here. Take a step forward. The water is as warm as your skin. You won't even feel it rushing over you. Come be with us. There is nothing left for you, nothing to worry about, nothing at all. Please rest with us. Please just stop breathing.

Angie felt the voice in her bones, a vibration that soothed the pain in her mind and brought an ice cold sting to her mid-section. She wanted to believe the voice. She wanted to step into the river and let it carry her like driftwood until her body rested against a mossy bank. She was sure she could listen to the sound of the water and tune out the sound of her heart until it ceased to bother her.

She could just let go. She was tired. Tired of running. Tired of fighting this thing that was inside her, this voice and these visions that had crawled into her blood. It couldn't just be acid. This voice was singing to her inside her skin.

Yes. Let go. Let go. Let go.

There was a new hunger to it she'd never felt before. It gave her the feeling that the river water was concealing something darker, that perhaps she would take one step in and sink like a stone.

Let go.

As much as Angie feared the river, she took a step toward it and wondered, *Even if I do find agony there, how long would it last? How bad could it be? How long could I hurt before my mind would finally shut off and allow me to rest?*

The toes of her left foot dipped into the water. It was warm, perfectly warm, like she imagined the temperature of her blood.

She took a step forward. Her submerged right foot became icy cold; it was numb in seconds. The voice came in through the cold.

YES YES YES YES YOU ARE WITH US ALWAYS WITH US NOW.

I'm nothing. It was her own last thought before she submitted to the hungry voice and fell forward into the water.

She tasted cold black river water and felt her own hands wrap around her throat and squeeze. Her eyes opened under the surface of the river and she saw something moving in the black beneath her. The river was too deep. Something was surfacing to claim her, moving quickly on an icy current. Her hands wrapped even tighter around her throat. Something wrapped around her waist, squeezing tight, dragging her down. She tasted her own blood in the water.

There's too much pain here. Her own thought was shattered by the voice, it's pitch cold and demanding.

WITH US IN US IN US IN US INSIDE US.

No! She tried to unwrap her hands from her own throat. They were no longer her own, and had become fixed, like a ring of petrified wood, tight around her neck.

The river had her.

LET GO. YOUR LINE HAS FALLEN. ALL BLOOD LOST. ALL WILL BE FORGIVEN. SHE WILL BE WITH US SOON.

Kaya? She's my blood. She's one of us.

Us?

It's talking about my whole family.

YES YES YES. SHE WILL FOLLOW LIKE YOU HAVE FOLLOWED. NO OTHER CHOICES.

Angie's hands squeezed tighter, her chest hitched and fought for air as she was dragged deeper.

YOU WILL ALL SLEEP THE LAST OF YOU DEAD LIKE YOU WANTED LIKE WE DREAMED.

Angie pictured Kaya as a baby, floating in the water before her, gray eyes staring back. She pictured her child sinking, stone heavy, into the black beneath her.

And the anger returned like a fire in her bones, turning her skeleton to forged steel.

Her hands became her own; she unleashed them from her throat and screamed into the black water.

"You can never have her!"

That which pulled her down slipped loose. Angie felt her body lifting up to the surface of the river and breaking into the air. She continued to rise, an upward spiral of consciousness that brought her back into her flesh.

She was back on the mattress, naked, furious, and alone. Angie moved her hands gingerly toward her throat, through which she could barely pull a thin stream of air. She touched her neck and found the skin didn't feel bruised, but the inside of her throat felt dangerously swollen. She tried with difficulty to breathe slow and fill her lungs, but could barely pull enough air in to keep her head steady.

Angie quieted her breath when she heard footsteps in the hall— *Is it "Uncle Curtis," Cypher, a burglar? Am I awake, asleep, alive?*—and although she was nearly asphyxiated, she did not breathe again until she heard the sound of the front door slamming closed. The sound reverberated through the walls of the old house.

Angie remembered how Colleen used to run from the house at the ragged end of barbiturate benders, slamming the front door so hard that the pictures on Angie's walls vibrated. When Colleen slammed the door like that, it usually meant that Angie wouldn't be seeing her for a couple of days. Angie hadn't missed her then;

Colleen's absence had always brought a sense of peace to the house, even though Angie was often left to fend for herself with little in the cupboards.

Angie found, upon waking in the strange room that didn't feel like home, that she wished it *was* Colleen who had slammed the door just now. Then she could run to the front yard and catch the old woman and ask her what the hell was going on.

But Colleen was dead. And Kaya was missing. And Angie could feel her heartbeat at the back of her skull. She knew there were no answers, but she also knew that to fall back to sleep right now would mean death. It would mean meeting the thing or things at the bottom of the river.

Angie opened her eyes.

Her head throbbed as she sat up, and the fading daylight that snuck in beneath the window blinds gave the room a strange glow. It was as if the world had turned gray. Angie wondered if the blow to her head had left her color-blind, but the bedroom door showed a hint of brown that comforted her worry. She let her eyes focus on the door, an attempt to re-orient her sight. The wood whorls swirled together, running over each other like liquid. Then a long face with black eyes emerged from the shapes of the wood grain and stared through her.

"Get out of my head!" she shouted. Then she turned away.

I can fight this. As long as I don't accept it, it can't hurt me.

Angie thought back to the very real pain of the rose thorns emerging from her skin, of how empty and close to death she'd felt when she was rooted to the soil in the forest and floating in the murk of the river.

But the river wasn't even real. I was in this room the whole time, and when I woke up I was hurting myself. None of it was real. Whatever this thing is that's after me, maybe it can't hurt me. It almost swallowed me in the woods and it's been following me ever since, waiting for me to collapse, give up, self-destruct. Maybe it's depending on me to hurt myself.

I'm not going to do that anymore—never again. I made it here and I'm alive. The forest can't have me.

She let her anger take over and cultivated it, pictured long-haired "Uncle Curtis" with his sick hands around Kaya's throat.

Is Kaya still alive?

Angie didn't know anymore. If Kaya was dead then Angie had nothing.

If she's gone, I'll find Colleen's pistol and kill Curtis, then kill myself if I have to. So long as I don't end up in the woods, with that pleading voice in my ear, sucking me dry.

She stood despite the steady throb in her skull. *Something has changed.* She was completely naked, but didn't remember taking off her underwear. She was fairly certain she had vomited on the mattress and soiled herself, but she was clean and the bed showed only a couple of damp spots.

Someone's been in this room with me.

Angie was out of the small stale room in seconds, horrified at the thought, feeling violated. She was comforted when nothing came dripping from between her legs.

Someone cleaned me after I was sick. What the fuck? None of Cypher's friends would avoid a free ride. They probably wouldn't even have cleaned me first, just hopped right on. God... how many days have I been asleep?

She felt an intense need to find clothing, to wrap herself up in something and feel safe. She walked up the stairs.

She hadn't been in Colleen's room for years. She wasn't surprised by the unmade bed, the tissues on the floor, the strewn clothing that covered the carpet. She grabbed a green sweatshirt and a pair of blue jeans from Colleen's closet and slid into them. They were tight, which meant Colleen had lost even more weight since Angie's last unexpected drop-in.

Angie searched under Colleen's bed for the old pistol she used to keep. It wasn't in its box, so Angie figured the old bat must have hawked it for pills.

As Angie slid out from under the bed she noticed an old glass of water sitting on Colleen's small, wooden nightstand. Angie could tell it was old because a thin layer of algae had grown green across its surface.

Angie lifted the cup, and then dropped it when she saw tiny eyes staring back at her.

The glass hit the shag carpet, water spilling out. Angie picked it back up and saw some sort of plant debris sitting waterlogged at the bottom of the empty cup. She threw the glass against the wall, and found the shattering sound satisfying.

Did the voice get Colleen, too? Did she see the trash turn human and moan? Did she see faces in the wood-grain? Maybe she took Kaya into the woods with her. Maybe they are out there right now with the wind whistling in their open mouths.

Fuming she walked from the room. The anger helped her as she searched the kitchen for a large knife. If "Uncle Curtis" or Cypher did come for her, she wanted to make sure they never touched her again. All she could find was a flimsy eight-inch steak knife, but it felt good in her right hand.

She felt even safer when she spotted Rusky's old fork lying in the hall. Its tines were dark red. The thing had probably saved her life. She put it in her left pocket.

Shit, I've got a fork and a knife. I'm more prepared for dinner than self-defense.

Still Rusky's fork felt warm even through the pocket of her jeans. It had saved her twice before, and it gave her a sense of pride to carry it.

I defended myself. I'm a fighter now.

Angie didn't know how much she felt like a fighter until the moment she entered the living room and looked out the front window and across the street.

She saw "Uncle Curtis" opening a car door. She saw Kaya stepping out of the car, so much older than the last time Angie had pretended to be her mother. Angie's heart ached for a second, filled with joy, an intense longing to hold her daughter, at last.

She's alive. Oh my God, she's alive!

And she's with him!

Angie was out the front door and across the street in seconds, running shoeless with the steak knife clenched in her right fist.

Kaya and the man who had attacked Angie were already inside when Angie hit the front door, but the man hadn't locked it. Angie threw the door open as hard as she could. It hit resistance and flew back at her, almost slamming into her face. She hit it again, this time with her right shoulder.

Fire filled the right side of her body. The shoulder she'd dislocated in the woods burned with new agony, and the door still didn't open, although there was now yelling from behind it. She could hear the voices of both her daughter and "Uncle Curtis" raised in shock. Angie pressed harder against the door with her left shoulder. She yelled through the crack in the door.

"Open this fucking door. Open it *right-Goddamned-now* or I swear to God I'll gut you from head to toe. Open it. Fucking open it. Please, God, open this door. Let me have my daughter."

Angie heard Kaya's voice from the other side of the door. "What's she talking about Curtis? Is that my mom?"

Angie yelled back. "Yes, Kaya, it's me, it's Angie—I mean, it's Mom—and I need you to help me get this door open right now."

She heard the man speaking to her daughter, grunting as he strained to keep the door closed to Angie. "Kaya, I can't open it. This woman is crazy. I don't know that she's really you're mother. She wants to hurt us."

Angie couldn't believe it. She groaned, "No. No. No." She pressed harder against the door and this time it almost yielded. She caught a glimpse of Kaya's face, wet with tears, before the man pressed harder and almost sealed her out.

"Do you want to hurt me?" Kaya asked.

The question tore at Angie, to hear it from her own daughter's lips. It hurt because it was a fair question. She could no longer deny that she'd born resentment for the girl since the moment Peter walked away.

Angie answered as calmly as she could, her voice trembling.

"No. Never, honey. Please just let me in. Uncle Curtis, please just let me in."

A man's voice, scared, trembling. "I can't. You're going to kill me."

"No, I won't kill you. Just back away from the door and put your hands above your head. I need to see my daughter."

"No way, lady, I can't do that. How do I know you're even her mother?"

Angie felt sick at the question. How could she prove she was Kaya's mother? They had no real shared memories. They had no special times together. They were blood, they were family, and that was all they had between them. She was Kaya's mother on a purely animal level.

"I don't know. Just let me in, or I'll call the cops and they'll let me in."

"The cops?"

Angie sensed fear in his question, thought she could smell his panic-sweat through the crack in the door. She played it for all she had.

"Yeah, I'll call the cops and they'll arrest you for kidnapping and assault, and I'll have Kaya back anyway. But you don't want that, so play smart and open the fucking door right now."

It was Kaya who grabbed the doorknob. Angie could hear her talking to Curtis. "Let her in. Please."

The door swung open, and Angie faced the man and her daughter. Kaya's arms were wrapped around Uncle Curtis' waist. Both of them were shaking, afraid, ready to run.

Kaya spoke quietly, pleading. "Please don't hurt us, Angie."

Angie let the knife slip from her hand and walked in the front door.

10—The Domestics

They stood in Curtis' living room, unmoving, not looking at each other. The tension and silence was so oppressive that Curtis desperately wanted to break it, but couldn't think of anything appropriate to say. Finally he backed away with his eyes on Angie and sat in his easy chair. Angie turned toward Kaya, but the girl was already walking toward the couch. Kaya sat at one end of the couch and Angie moved slowly to sit at the other end.

Curtis decided that the fact that Angie had dropped the knife when Kaya had pleaded with her meant that she was not an immediate threat to the safety of his family. But the future? Time would tell.

Did he have it in him, he wondered, to eliminate the threat if he had to?

Angie was the first to speak. Her voice was slight and it trembled. She asked Kaya a lot of questions—Are you okay? Do you know who I am?—but offered no information about herself. Kaya answered her questions emotionlessly and without making eye-contact.

She's just beachcombing, Curtis thought as he watched Angie, though at first he didn't know why he thought that.

As a child Curtis had been fascinated with the ocean, but it wasn't until he was twenty years old that he'd seen it for the first and only time in his life. As he stood on the beach, trying to absorb the immensity of it and feel the power of its waves on the shore, he saw a group of scuba divers make their way out into the water from a rocky prominence. He wished he could do that, to really experience the ocean, but it frightened him; to think of himself, such a small creature, being swallowed up by a vast and powerful life form. It might kill him.

He turned away, deciding to settle for finding something to remind him of the ocean. He'd taken a pretty shell. *But a shell was all it was*, he thought.

He'd been afraid to dive in. Curtis now saw the same apprehension in Angie. Some things were just too huge.

Curtis could tell Angie was upset with the response she was getting from Kaya even though she was trying to hide it. He felt sorry for her although Angie deserved no better.

Everything that washes up on the beach is dead. It's not like diving into the ocean and seeing everything alive.

"Angie, tell her something about yourself," Curtis suggested.

Somewhat irritated, she turned to him. Then she was quiet for a time and turned back to Kaya and said, "I would not have been a good mother for you in the past, but I'd like to try to become one now."

Kaya shrugged her shoulders and got up and went to the bathroom.

"That's not exactly what I meant," Curtis said.

He got up and went into his bedroom to look in the mirror and check on his fork wound. His cheek was swollen, but the four tiny holes were closing up.

One inch higher and I'd be missing an eye.

Curtis went into the kitchen to fix them all some dinner. As he moved about preparing the meal, he tried to listen for footsteps—he didn't want Angie sneaking up on him. He didn't know what to do about the present situation. He was glad Kaya's presence had calmed Angie, but he didn't know how to feel about Angie being in his house. He'd never expected that Angie might turn up or even care what happened to her daughter.

Was that why you thought you could get away with claiming Kaya? he asked himself. *No, I'm not trying to get away with anything.*

All he could think of to do was to follow through with his plans for the weekend: Making his house into a home for Kaya.

Miss Martinez had visited four days ago to make sure Kaya was doing well and that the girl's living situation was adequate. She hadn't been impressed by the meager, gray-shaded room that

Curtis had prepared for Kaya. Curtis could tell from the blank look on her face that she didn't approve. She had called Kaya's room "barely adequate." Barely adequate had sounded like failure to Curtis. He vowed to himself that by the next visit Kaya's room would be a princess' palace. Anything to keep the police from looking for alternate housing for his angel.

He couldn't stand the thought of Kaya in a foster home.

He was glad he wouldn't have to pack Kaya off to school for the next two days. If Kaya was the way into Angie's heart, Curtis didn't want to be without her until he knew if he could trust the woman not to hurt him again.

POLICE ➤ ⋙ DO NOT CROSS

Angie walked into the kitchen as Curtis was adding the browned hamburger to the spaghetti sauce he was making.

"Why do you even care?" Angie asked, acid in her tone. "What are you up to?"

Curtis craned his neck to look out into the living room. Where was Kaya? He didn't want her to hear this.

Angie seemed to pick up on his concern. "She's still in the bathroom."

Curtis relaxed a bit.

"Are you a pervert? Do you get off on little girls?"

Curtis could feel himself going red in the face. Before Angie recognized it as shame, he would convince her the color came from anger. "Your mother thought so," he said, reminding himself to keep his voice down so Kaya wouldn't hear him. Even so, he was spitting as he continued. "She offered Kaya to me if I would keep mowing her goddamn lawn. How's that for good parenting? I told her to go to hell."

Angie turned away, and Curtis realized that he really was angry, that he'd meant what he said and that, though he'd had plenty of fantasies, he'd never had any intention of having sex with Kaya. He would never do that to her.

"You left Kaya with that sick old woman."

Angie nodded her head. "How did Colleen die?" Her voice was low, defeated, her eyes fixed on the floor.

"The night I told her to go to hell, she shot herself in the fucking head. I felt guilty as hell, but I wanted to do all I could to protect Kaya. What have you ever done for her?" He knew he needed to tone it down now or Angie might become dangerous. He wanted no more of that.

"I see what you're doing for Kaya," Angie said, still not looking up. "I've seen the room you made for her. I never did anything like that for her. And I know you don't have to do that stuff. So what are you after? I mean, do you think you can get Colleen's money? 'Cause that's a laugh. C'mon—everybody's after something."

Yeah, he was after something—someone to care about, a family. But how could he explain that without sounding like a weirdo?

He didn't respond to her question, but he'd noticed a softening in her eyes. He was about to try and explain himself when she spoke again, this time in a quieter voice.

"Wish I'd had somebody like you around when I was growing up, someone to keep me away from Colleen," Angie said.

Was that an apology? She was expressing appreciation for what he'd done for Kaya. That was something.

Angie's mouth continued to move after her voice stopped. Curtis could almost make out the syllables, but no sound came out. There was fear in her eyes.

"Did you hear that?" she asked, turning wide, desperate eyes to him.

Fucking great, Curtis thought, *now she's having a psychotic episode. Probably best to ignore it.*

"Get the mushrooms out of the crisper," he said, "and wash them for me."

Angie seemed to relax and she moved to do as he asked.

As long as Angie isn't dangerous, I have to care about what she thinks when it comes to Kaya. She is Kaya's mother. If she trusts me with her daughter, maybe she'll learn to love me too.

CAUTION - CAUTION - CAUTION -

That night Curtis allowed Angie to sleep in his room while he took the sofa. He hoped she'd sleep naked in his bed. In a half-asleep state, he heard strange voices in muffled blurts and gasps coming from his bedroom. He fell deeper into sleep and dreamed Angie had seen countless whispering strangers at her window and invited them into her bed.

POLICE LINE DO NOT CROSS

On Saturday morning they went to Houarner's Department Store to buy furniture and other material for Kaya's new bedroom. Kaya clung to Curtis during most of the shopping spree, walking up and down the aisles right next to the shopping cart he was pushing, or hugging his waist when they were not in motion. Angie asked her what colors she liked, what style of furniture she might prefer. She held up one stuffed animal after another to see if her daughter might respond favorably, but Kaya was as quiet and withdrawn as usual.

Curtis knew she was trying hard to be a real mother. The way she went about it was strangely endearing despite Kaya's lack of interest.

He began to see that everything he'd ever seen as attractive in Kaya was there in Angie. Her ass looked good in those tight little sweat pants too. The shirt he'd loaned her looked good filled out with her tits. Being too large for her, she'd tied the shirt tails in front so that her nice flat stomach and belly button showed. He liked the idea that later he would be able to put on the shirt that had touched her breasts. He had already decided to put it aside after she took it off so it wouldn't get washed before he could smell it and put it on.

She was still getting nowhere with Kaya. Finally Angie became despondent and sat down on a child's bed in the furniture department.

Curtis sat down next to her and tried to think of something to say. Kaya wandered over to the next aisle.

"I'm nothing to her," Angie said quietly so that only Curtis could hear her. "I came back here to make sure she was safe. But she's got you now. She doesn't need me."

"I don't think they're going to let me keep her." Curtis hadn't intended to admit that to Angie—hell, he didn't want to admit it to himself, but somehow he couldn't help it. He'd had fantasies about going off with Kaya, disappearing, both of them taking on new identities and living out their lives together somewhere. Just then he knew it was only a dream—they'd never get away with it. The authorities would never stop looking for her. If Kaya was going to be family, then he would have to be seen by her and, he supposed, by Angie as family. He knew now that he'd have to earn that.

"You and Kaya... well... that will take time," Curtis said. "You can both stay with me for a while if you want."

Angie didn't respond, so he didn't push it.

He tried to see the three of them as a nuclear family, but the image it conjured was more apocalyptic than what he'd been shooting for.

"This shopping thing—let me show you how it's done," Curtis said. He loaded their shopping cart with colorful bed clothes, curtains, stuffed animals, toys and a few books.

While Curtis was picking things out he noticed that Kaya followed along beside Angie and looked at her once or twice. Angie blew it by turning her attention to the girl and trying to talk to her. Kaya retreated, standing off on her own until the shopping was done.

Curtis found a clerk and ordered a canopy bed, shelves, a dresser and mirror and asked for them to be delivered to his address by the end of the day. He paid for everything and they left the store.

On the way home, he saw Kaya smile once or twice. He knew that Angie saw it too.

Angie was very sexy when she smiled.

CAUTION - CAUTION - CAUTION - CAUTION - CAUTION -

In the afternoon, Curtis and Angie hauled everything out of Kaya's room and painted the walls and ceiling, waited two hours and then gave them another coat.

Then the furniture arrived from Houarner's.

While Kaya hugged her pillow and watched from the doorway, Angie and Curtis set up Kaya's new room, moving the furniture into place, arranging toys and books, hanging the curtains and making the bed.

Kaya looked worried. Curtis put it out of his mind.

POLICE LINE DO NOT CROSS

Again in the night, while Curtis was drifting off to sleep on the couch, he heard voices coming from his bedroom. This time he had the impression they came from somewhere deep in the earth itself, somewhere in the shadows.

Sunday morning Kaya sat next to Angie at the breakfast table and asked her what she liked to eat for breakfast.

Angie clearly didn't know what to say. People who lived the way Angie did, Curtis thought, probably didn't eat much breakfast, let alone have much choice. Angie started to say something then stopped, perhaps afraid she might scare her daughter away again.

Kaya turned away, got up from the table and went to the bathroom.

"She hates me for abandoning her," Angie said.

"She doesn't even know you. How can she hate you?"

Angie's mouth moved as if she were responding to Curtis, but nothing came out. She seemed surprised, a bit frightened and embarrassed. She buried her face in her hands.

POLICE 🎗 ᐳᐃᓭ DO NOT CROSS

Sunday afternoon Curtis cleaned house in anticipation of Miss Martinez's inspection the next day. Angie helped out here and there. Afterward Curtis relaxed in his easy chair and read a book for about an hour and a half. Kaya was taking a nap in her new room.

Curtis put his book down when Angie entered the living room with a fist full of papers and an angry look on her face. She was holding his print-outs on the Smith family. He had given her the run of the house, but he didn't expect she'd go through his stuff.

"What the fuck is this?"

"I wanted to know about our family."

"What do you mean *our* family?"

"I mean *your* family," Curtis said, and it hurt a little when he said it. "I found all that stuff online, on genealogy sites."

Angie looked horrified. "You didn't just make this stuff up? This shit is real?"

As he nodded his head, Curtis could see some of the more outrageous stories from his notes reflected in her eyes.

"No way is this one about the swamp lady true."

"Oh, yeah, the one about Margaret Smith."

The web site Curtis had taken the story from said that during the Civil War Margaret Smith had lured soldiers on both sides to her home in the Ghost River Swamp of Tennessee to become food for her and her children."

"She fucking ate people?" Angie asked.

The site claimed that all the men of Margaret Smith's "back-woods" family had died at the battle of Shys Hill in Nashville and she was desperate for some way to provide for her youngsters.

"Well, yes. It was for her family. Surely you can understand that." He regretted saying it even as he spoke the words.

"No, I can't."

Neither could her neighbors, Curtis thought.

When the nearby community of Bardsville got wind—literally—of what was going on in the Ghost River Swamp and went to investigate, they found at least fourteen corpses in and around the Smith cabin, tangled in the brush, or half submerged and rotting in a fetid morass that surrounded the property. Those who discovered the scene said that in some cases they couldn't tell where corpse left off and vegetation began. They burned the cabin and the imme-

diate area around it before a final determination of the number of dead could be made.

But then there were plenty of other Smith family weirdoes listed in those pages. The entries concerning the countless murder victims, murderers, rapists, child molesters and necrophiliacs were among the tamest.

"Yes, but it's not as bad as it sounds," Curtis said, trying to think of something reassuring to say.

"What are you talking about? How could it be any worse? This is some of the weirdest shit I've ever read, and you're telling me it's about my family? No fucking wonder I can't make it in this world."

"There are probably lots of mistakes in the records. It's not like your family name is rare or anything, and you can't believe everything you read."

"Yeah, but if half this shit is true...."

"It's just a bunch of stuff some of your family did," Curtis said. He was scrambling for something to say as he watched the light go out of Angie's eyes and that manic anger she held close crept into them. "It doesn't mean you have to be that way too. You have a choice."

"Yeah, sure I do."

"You can be okay. You're good like Kaya, you have to be. Everything I love in Kaya, I see in you too," he said desperately, but he knew he meant it.

Angie just stared at him blankly.

"Mama?" came Kaya's voice from the bedroom. Was she calling out in her sleep? "Will you come here?"

"Your daughter's calling for you. I think she really does need her mother."

Now Angie's transformation was complete—the animal fear was clear to see in her eyes and body language. "I can't take this shit anymore," she said hysterically and went into his room and shut the door.

An hour later, while Curtis and Kaya were fixing dinner, they heard a crashing sound come from his bedroom. When Curtis looked in on her, he found Angie had pulled the blinds off the window while trying to open them. She had found the pint of Bourbon he'd bought to celebrate the holidays with last year. Since he'd had no one to celebrate with, he hadn't cracked the seal on the bottle. Now it was empty, and Angie was sitting cross-legged on the floor with her head hanging down.

Curtis wasn't surprised when she raised her head and stared at him with hate in her eyes. The same ugliness that had hovered behind Colleen's dull stare was now filling the room, slowly and heavily, unrestrained.

Angie spoke. "Get away from me you fucking creep."

She grabbed the empty bourbon bottle and lifted it above her head.

He quickly closed the door before the glass hit the wood. He heard the shattered pieces crash to the floor.

He walked back out to the kitchen, expecting to find Kaya there. Water was boiling on the stove unattended, steam twirling.

Curtis found Kaya in the living room, pushing his thin blinds aside, looking out the window. She turned at the sound of his footfalls.

"Curtis, whose car is that?"

"Which car, Kaya?"

"The big white one parked in the driveway of my old house."

11—Swallowing

Angie's belly burned and tore at itself, clenching under the barrage of bourbon she'd downed faster than she could control. Her world was spinning but it wouldn't go black. Color had leaked out of the world and the whole room wavered before her, a swimming gray. Even the pale moonlight coming through her window felt artificial, cold and fake.

They were right. The voices were right. I've fought for nothing. Earned nothing. Kaya isn't even mine.

GHOST WHEN SHE WAS BORN QUIET NOW QUIET UNDERSTAND FEEL AND FALL FALL QUIET.

The voice was steady now, a force of nature like gravity sucked up inside her skull. Even through the booze, her eyes watered at the pain.

Even if I fight....

SEED SPILLS BLOOD SPILLS OVER AND OVER UNTIL QUIET PLEASE NOW JUST NEVER.

Oh... even if I fight, there's nothing for her. The whole family, every one of us is wrong.

ALL OTHER THAN OTHER UNTIL SOFT AND APART CRUMBLING.

What did I think I could do? I'm not a mother. Running always felt right. I never even should have had her. Now she'll be like me.

YOU WILL ALL SLEEP.

Angie winced at the sound of the voice. It was so sure now that she was listening, so confident that her resolve had collapsed.

It was right.

She swayed in her cross-legged position on the floor and stead-ied herself with one hand. She squeezed her eyes shut as tight as she could, as if she could shut her eyes on the world forever. Just disappear. No body for Kaya and Curtis to find. No proof that Angie had tried to crawl her way into their strangely normal life.

She felt the voice inside her, staring into her heart, trespassing on the things that should only be known to her. Listening to every-thing. It knew her.

It knew she was ready to let go. The voice turned to whisper again.

You can disappear with us. You can be warm. You'll never be alone.

Was the voice really that bad? Had Angie really felt so afraid when she'd embraced it? Maybe this thing that had crawled under her skin was right. It felt so close to her own thoughts, her own doubts.

We are in you. With you.

Maybe the voice was something good, some clean thing that culled her sick family away from the earth. Angie remembered being pulled beneath the surface of the river. Giving in hadn't felt right. It felt like being eaten alive. And each time she got close to giving in, thoughts and visions of Kaya had saved her.

Where is she now? My daughter. My angel. She's just another sick girl like me. No love for anyone else. I was wrong to expect more.

The world was wrong to you. You can be with us. Quiet now.

Part of Angie wanted to fight the voice, to fight for the affec-tion of her daughter, to fight against everything that had kept her from having the life she had tried to earn before Cypher pushed his sick, acid-soaked tongue into her mouth. *I can be a good mother. I can make our family right. I can fight.* That part of her fought to be heard, but the voice was rooted so deep inside her, so deep... and it felt stronger now, as if it were knitting the air tightly around her, making her movements slow and heavy.

The light from the bedroom window was brighter now, beam-ing in through the gray.

We are waiting for you. Be with us.

Unsteady, Angie rose to her feet. She reached her hand out to the window and felt a chill trickle through her sweating, drunken body. She knew she could push the window open and crawl out. She could walk silent into the woods behind the suburbs and disap-

pear.

She was distorting her daughter by being there.

Maybe Kaya's got a chance if I go now. Maybe it's not too late for her.

She steadied her shaking hand and pushed it closer to the glass. The cold from the other side of the window was numbing her arm. Even with the bourbon, her resolve wavered.

I'm going to be eaten alive. I will be sucked dry and disappear. She felt eyes on her skin from every direction. Eyes inside of her, studying every cell of her, wondering which pieces of her to pluck away first.

The anger she'd turned against the voice so many times now commanded her surrender.

Fucking do it. Open the window. Go. Get away from this place. You're not Kaya's savior. Do what you'd always wished Colleen would do. Just wander off.

A smaller fading voice in her head begged her to stay. She didn't listen.

As Angie pushed the window open, she felt the evening wind slide across her skin, bringing with it the odor of decaying leaves.

I'm going to die.

Before she had the window completely open she saw light spreading across the room, yellow light spilling in from the opening bedroom door. She couldn't avoid the thought that entered her mind although it reeked of the hope she'd fought to shed.

Oh, it's Kaya. She's come to pull me back before it's too late, to hold me and tell me she loves me and push this thing from my head. It's Kaya.

She turned her head rapidly. Her vision sloshed into place and she blinked to steady her sight and let her eyes adjust to the light. She could see only a shape moving toward her.

The silhouette was too large. The footsteps were too heavy.

"Kaya?"

There was no answer from the shape, only a swift motion that brought steel smacking against her skull.

She felt herself bounce once when she hit the carpet, the impact driving the air from her chest. Then she heard the voice.

"Hey, O'Rourke, I found this sorry bitch. She says the kid's name is Kaya. Shit, I'd forgotten. I couldn't forget *your* name though, Angie. It's about all I've had in my head since last time I saw you."

She felt a heavy steel-toed boot slam into her ribcage just as she was regaining her breath.

"Yeah, Angie, I've got to get you out of my mind. I think we're gonna have to split up."

She heard him spitting before she felt the warm saliva rolling off her cheek. She didn't reach up to wipe it away. She was afraid any movement would prompt another kick, and her chest was aching for a single breath.

Angie finally inhaled to the sound of a pistol being cocked above her head and in the distance, the sound of her daughter's scream muffled by flesh.

"Get up, bitch. We're getting out of here." Cypher sounded so happy.

O'Rourke's voice came from the other room. "Why can't we just do it here?"

Cypher was short with him, his breath clipped and controlled beneath his present rage. "Because if that guy on the floor isn't the *only* one that lives here, we'll have some unwanted visitors. I don't want any complications. Besides, the stuff is back at her mom's house. I want to have some fun with this. I think it's going to mean something this time, O'Rourke. I think I'm going to understand. I know this girl. Her eyes will tell me more."

Angie felt the steel muzzle against the top of her head.

"C'mon, Angie. Get up. We're going home."

As they were marched across the street at gunpoint, the suburbs of Monahan were quiet. *To each his own* was the law of the suburban sprawl. Angie felt surrounded and alone at the same time. Kaya walked quietly beside her, her head bowed.

Angie still hoped a neighbor would see them as they walked their tiny death march to Colleen's house. She looked back at Cypher, saw fire in his deep-set eyes, flecks of blood on his white-t-shirt, blue jeans, and boots.

She looked ahead to O'Rourke, saw that he'd copped Cypher's style and was sporting the same shaven-headed, neo-Nazi asshole look. There was no place for either of them to hide their pistols, so they let their arms hang straight to their sides and walked with only their legs moving.

Just out for a friendly stroll. Another lovely evening in Monahan.

She'd seen Curtis, or what was probably now just his body, sprawled in his living room. His neck was bent at a wrong angle, and his head and the carpet surrounding it were soaked red. She'd lost her belly upon seeing him; she'd dropped to the floor like a dog and puked out the bourbon she'd stolen from Curtis. She felt instantly sober, but she didn't know if it was the purging or the fear. Cool beads of sweat trickled across her flushed forehead. Cypher had been frustrated with her.

"Get up. Get up now, you fucking whore."

Jealous. He sounded jealous, this same guy who had pimped her out for cheap thrills and raped her in the woods. He thought she was sick at the sight of Curtis, that she was overwrought and had dropped to the floor at the sight of another man's fallen body.

Was he right? She didn't know. She didn't hate Curtis. She didn't know what she felt. Things were too fucked for her to have a straight-forward emotion.

Angie saw Cypher's old white Cadillac parked out front of Colleen's. The trunk was open, but the guys marched her and Kaya right past the greasy old ride and up to the front door.

Come home. You can end now.

The voice never left her. It was just a matter of degrees.

Even with the anger she felt now, being torn from the quiet death she sought and attacked by Cypher, watching her daughter shake with fear while some asshole had a gun pointed at her back, the voice was still digging away at her.

It's like fate. It's like being able to hear fate.

Angie watched her daughter's small shaking hand reach out and slowly open the front door to Colleen's house.

She hasn't even looked back at me. Even now, I'm nothing to her. She thinks Curtis was the only one who could protect her. She's afraid and thinks she's alone. Where's her Uncle Curtis now?

It was then that she felt the icy chill run through her belly and knew that her visions hadn't ended. The fear, the knowledge that her daughter could soon die, opened her up and the voice was wrapped around her sight again.

The world is wrong to you. All of you. You will end soon.

Angie smelled garbage and hot moist earth wafting up from behind her. As they entered the house she heard the sloshing of old food against plastic, hollow cans clunking together. She knew that if she turned and looked at Cypher and O'Rourke, they would not be human. They would be things, human in shape, reeking of discarded fat, shambling on slick plastic-bag- limbs, stuffed with rubbish, yard debris, and perhaps rotting bits of old enemies.

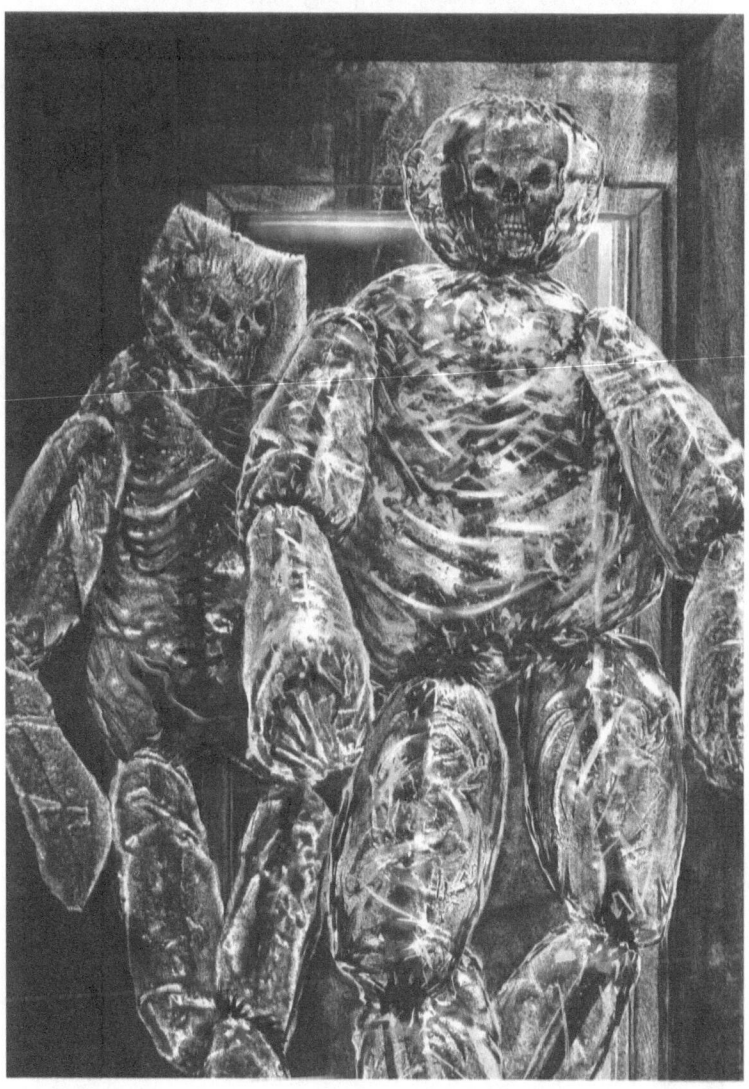

Cypher was inches behind Angie and urging her forward with his left hand at her lower back. She couldn't turn and look at him, but she saw his shadow through the rainbow-edged periphery of her sight and heard his voice, a cold reptile tone, the sound of a falling stone.

"Get in the living room, cunt. Don't turn on any lights. Don't fuck around. I'm having a hard time not shooting you on the spot, so don't think you've got any sympathy cards to play."

"Okay, Cyph."

"*Okay, Cyph. Okay, Cyph.*" His voice was high and mocking. "Jesus, I seriously cannot stand the sound of your voice anymore. You sound so weak, Angie."

She felt weak. She felt afraid. She'd been fighting something she couldn't beat for so long that she didn't know if she could struggle anymore.

I have to struggle. I have to fight. They're going to kill us both. Maybe I can... what—what can I do?

Her sense of helplessness fueled the voice. She could feel it swirling rapid in her blood.

"Sit down. Now. Over by Kaya."

Kaya was already sitting on the old living room couch, her right hand on the armrest. There was a shell-shocked look in her eyes that said none of this was registering as real to her.

Maybe this will just be a nightmare for her, a quick nightmare that she won't wake up from....

ALL REST QUIET NOW JUST END.

The voice whipsawed through her skull again, hungry, angry, like it was losing something if Angie gave in this way. Angie hated it and knew then that she would always hate it, that she could never really give herself to something that so badly wanted her to stop being.

"SHUT UP!"

Kaya seized the armrest tight at the sound of her mother's cry. Even Cypher and O'Rourke were a little shaken by it, but then Cypher began to laugh.

He raised his gun and pointed it at Angie before speaking.

"Oh...oh, Jesus, Angie. Jesus, just sit down there on the couch...."

She sat to the left and didn't reach her hand out for Kaya. She was nothing to the girl. She'd lost that much and tried to accept it though it still hurt.

Cypher was still laughing, a dry raspy laugh that was heavy with both contempt and amusement. His face looked bone-thin in the dark living room, his t-shirt and blue jeans appeared gray in the streetlight that filtered through Colleen's drapes. "You're still tripping, huh? I mean, I knew you were frying hard that night in the woods, you had to have been, after what you did to me with that lighter. After all the love I gave you. And then I find you shacked up with some old dude with bad hair who thinks he can stop me from doing what I want."

Angie spoke without thinking. "I wasn't shacked up with him. He was just some guy, some old pervert that we were staying with until I got my head on straight."

She didn't know why she had said it, but she knew it didn't feel true. And Kaya had reacted to the comment, shifting in her seat, putting her hands in her lap and dropping her head. The movement must have spooked O'Rourke because he too had his gun raised now, leveled at Kaya.

Cypher turned to O'Rourke, his head snapping cobra-quick, his neck muscles ridged and shadowy in the thin living room light. Angie saw that his jaw muscles were clenched tight before he spoke and that he was grinding his teeth between words as was O'Rourke.

They're tweeking. They're amped and I can't even get angry at the man pointing a gun at my daughter. I should be fighting. I should be standing between the gun and Kaya. This can't be happening. Fight.

WRONG WRONG WRONG QUIET ACCEPT SLOW FALL.

"Hey, O'Rourke," Cypher said, "drop your fucking gun and chill for a second. That bugged out little bitch isn't going to do anything. She's just like her mama bear. She's a good little bitch. Isn't that right, Kaya?"

Kaya said nothing.

O'Rourke looked anxious, ready to get down to business.

God, what business do they have with us? Just murder? Something worse?

Angie remembered the blood she'd seen on Cypher's shell-toed sneakers about a month ago. She'd remembered his words, how he'd been looking for something, some sort of understanding. He understood murder though, of that much, she was sure. So how else could he learn from them?

Pain thresholds? The taste of flesh? Secrets in our screams?

Cypher didn't seem to want those things, at least not right away.

He'd set up this fucked up family meeting in the living room. If he wanted straight mayhem, he'd just do it.

ALL QUIET UNDERNEATH HERE AND NOW BRING HER.

Angie winced again, a puff of breath escaping her nose. She could feel Cypher's attention snap in her direction.

The voice had confused her.

"Bring who?" she asked into the distance, the space between her head and the floor.

"Holy shit, Angie! You have snapped. You have totally lost it. I figured after what you pulled with Rusky, that maybe you had your shit together. Rusky said you robbed him with a fucking fork. I mean, Hey-soos Christo, Angie, that's some weird shit. First you set my balls on fire, then you come after Rusky all primal. Anti-social shit, Angie."

Angie had to work as hard as she could to not look at the shape of the fork in her sweat-pants pocket when he mentioned it. It seemed dangerous to let him know she had anything, even that old fork. She hadn't stopped carrying it since that day.

"What are you getting at, Cyph?" O'Rourke sounded pissy, and had begun tapping his right toe.

"Shut up, Rourky. I'm just talking with my old lady. Trying to figure out where she went. This bitch here…" He pointed at her with his pistol. "I'm not really sure who she is. She's gone worse than anybody else who had that acid."

Angie lifted her head toward Cypher, suddenly very interested in what he had to say.

"Oh, you don't know, do you? Can you believe that Rourky? She doesn't know about the bad fry. Classic. Well, while you were off in the woods and I was being carted to the hospital, a couple of other kids went loco off the acid that was out there that night. I saw the shit on the news later, while they pumped me full of morphine and debated about cutting my dick off. Third degree burns, Angie, that's serious shit. And by the way…."

He stepped forward and smacked her across the face with his pistol before she had a second to dodge the attack. Her left cheek tore wide, blood running hot over her face. She heard Kaya yelp, a momentary respite from her shocked stupor. Angie sat back up quickly and pushed the sleeve of her sweatshirt to her cheek.

"God that felt good. Anyway, Angie, two other kids out there couldn't handle their doses that night. It's probably some crooked Rainbow Fam shit. That hippy stuff always goes bad, man. The kids, this couple, they went back to their tent, and they must have been seeing some crazy shit, 'cause they gouged each other's eyes out. They said the guy's left thumb actually broke into her skull and was up in her brain. They both died, and the media played it up all tragic and graphic and shit to put the scare into the other youths out there who could be contemplating chasing the Big Never Never on some LSD." Cypher laughed. Angie could tell he was high off the sound of his own voice.

O'Rourke piped in, smiling. "The guy actually bit his own tongue off and choked on it."

"Yeah," Cypher continued, "it was some ill shit. You got the same doses and tried to set me on fire. It takes some serious L to make people act like that, to free them from themselves that much. I didn't know how good the shit was when I bought it. I thought it was just for kicks, you know, catch a little buzz then put you on the same train, see if we could work something out. But the doses were too much. That fry, Angie...."

He paused, shaking his head in disbelief. She felt anger warming her body, making her more lucid. If Cypher hadn't bought that acid and forced it on her... He'd left her defenseless to the voice, to herself.

"That fry is so good, Angie. It's a window, man, a window onto *something*. IT talks to you, you know; it shows you who you are; it just takes all that shit inside your head and puts it right in front of your eyes and feeds it to you. It makes you understand. It helped me to understand why I'm here."

Angie took the bait, unable to avoid asking, too intrigued by the idea that anyone else might be having the same experiences she'd had.

"Why are you here, Cypher?"

He pulled a tiny bottle with an eye-dropper from the front right pocket of his jeans. It was half full of clear fluid.

"I'm here to help other people understand. To show them what they're worth, what's inside them, what they can become. O'Rourke's been helping me too, spreading the message. He helped Rusky."

Angie remembered Rusky's centipede, the fire that had been dropped into his eyes. She didn't feel any closer to tears, but she felt something inside her breaking.

"Rusky's problem was that he was always bug-fucking-crazy so the shit didn't work too well. Rusky wasn't a good boy. He wouldn't cough up my cash. He helped your sorry ass out, after you attacked him. He was our first try so we chalked it up to trial and error. I was pissed when Rusky held out so I sent my buddy Pearson out to see him.

"Pearson said Rusky had peeled half his upper thigh off by hand, and was working his fingers around in the big muscle on top. P-dog just about lost his belly at the sight of it, man. Said Rusky was talking a bunch of crazy shit about bugs and secrets. P-dog also said that once he started hitting Rusky, the crazy fuck started crying and saying your name, saying that you knew the secrets of his heart, that you knew about his plan.

"P-dog ended up feeding Rusky some pieces of broken glass, just to see if he could. Said the dude was so crazy that when he held the glass to his face, Rusky opened his mouth wide just like a little baby and started chewing. He swallowed the glass 'to wash the centipede out.' That's what he said. P-dog played a hunch and told him that you were the one that put the centipede inside him. Rusky started crying and mentioned that you might be headed home, crying that you lied to him, betrayed him.

"I really feel bad for Pearson, man. He can't get the sound of Rusky chewing that glass out of his head."

Angie hung her head now, silent, knowing that if she looked up at Cypher and O'Rourke's faces, they would be covered in lizard scales and leaves. Cypher's voice felt so close to the old whispers that filled her head. So wrong.

Cypher stepped forward and tucked his free hand under her chin.

"What do you say, babe? How about you and me and our friend here, how about we all have a little understanding?"

Angie allowed him to dose her without struggle. She hadn't owned her mind for a long time anyway. He could pour the entire eye-dropper's contents into her mouth for all she cared. She'd already gone through the looking glass; why not dig a little deeper? She had a feeling Cypher's *understanding* came at a mortal price anyway.

Maybe these doses will push me over an edge, take me to some place where I can fight and be strong again. Maybe I can still save Kaya.

She pictured her skin spreading, a new all black form made of obsidian emerging from her tattered former self. She pictured the new version of herself tearing these sick men limb from limb, their blood sinking into her new body and making it glow.

The hope kept crawling back in. She tried to ignore it. She tried to let go.

Kaya had become alert as Cypher and O'Rourke approached her. Her eyes went wide, and she curled up tight, as if she could ball up and be impervious. O'Rourke reached out to unlatch her hands from her legs. Kaya reacted quickly, swiping out with her fingers as if they were talons, opening the thin skin on the back of O'Rourke's free hand.

Angie heard O'Rourke's gun cock and yelled, "No!"

Cypher elbowed O'Rourke sharply and spat, "Simmer down, Rourky. We need to do this right. Hey, Angie, you want to help this little bitch understand she's got no choice? 'Cause O'Rourke would just as soon kill her. I know from past experience that he's got a short temper with kids. He always drops the kids first."

Angie turned to Kaya, hoping her presence carried enough currency to keep her daughter alive if only for moments.

"Hey, Kaya? Kaya, baby, this is very serious. I know you're scared and I know these men hurt Curtis, but they don't want to hurt you. They just need to give you some medicine."

Jesus, what am I? What am I doing?

Maybe she'll see something beautiful and then just die. Maybe the dose will be too much and she won't have to deal with this anymore. Please, God, save us.

"Kaya, please, for mommy."

Kaya's eyes became alive again, her head whipped toward Angie. "You're not my mother. Stay away from me!"

O'Rourke's patience broke. He grabbed Kaya's face with his free hand and sunk his large fingers in behind her jawbone, using her pressure-points to force her mouth wide open.

"That's a good little birdy."

Cypher was quick with the eye-dropper. Angie watched two drops fall into her daughter's mouth; she thought she saw them turn to black oil as they fell. Then O'Rourke forced her mouth shut and held it for a moment.

142   *Alan M. Clark & Jeremy Robert Johnson*

What have they done?

O'Rourke let go of her and Kaya lashed out again. O'Rourke caught her hand and gave it a quick twist back toward her body. There was a sound, thin bones crunching. Then Kaya screamed and the smell of fear on her breath floated into Angie's nose.

Angie was up off the couch, but just as quickly Cypher had his gun leveled at her head. "Whoa there, mama bear. Sit your ass down." Cypher turned his attention to O'Rourke.

Angie was surprised to see Cypher pulling O'Rourke away roughly.

"Christ, Rourky, fucking chill. Not yet, man. Not yet. Let them peak. Let them *understand*. Then we'll play."

O'Rourke chilled as instructed. Cypher was clearly the alpha-dog and his bark wasn't idle.

What if O'Rourke just wants to kill us quick? What if he's sick of Cypher, of the things they've been doing?

Angie looked across the room at the retreating O'Rourke. He was smiling, watching Kaya writhe in pain. No, O'Rourke was into this as much as Cypher was. No hope there. No begging for mercy killing.

The men with empty eyes and cocked pistols settled into the ratty La-Z-Boy chairs across the room. They watched and waited. Angie was able to brace herself. She understood something of what could be done, what one human could do to another. She put no limitations on what might happen to her.

But Kaya?

Angie looked over at her daughter who was now cradling her shattered wrist and crying softly.

Why should she ever have to know this? She's still pure. Maybe... maybe what? Can I kill her before they get to?

Angie felt Rusky's fork through the fabric of her pocket and wondered if she could plunge it into her daughter's neck.

If I was strong? If I was quick? Could I do it?

She looked over at her daughter again, and knew that it could never be her hand that ended Kaya's life. It was an act she was incapable of, even in mercy. The girl looked miles away, tiny and ancient like an Indian woman wrapped in a shawl, waiting for harvest moon.

The acid's kicking in. Shit. Think straight, think straight for once.

She had no chance to think. The men with the guns, the men

she felt like she had once known, but who now wanted to eat her alive, were up from their fluffy domestic chairs and walking toward her and her child, their sharp skulls and razor faces intent on cleaving her skin from bone and leaving her fragmented.

"Rourky, check the little one's eyes, see if she's ready. I doubt she could even figure out how to attack you now."

Angie could smell the mens' breath from across the room, like motor oil, semen, and old blood, all mixed up and heated in reptile engines, fed by an old black pulse.

O'Rourke tilted Kaya's head back. Angie watched him peer into her eyes, squinting. "Yeah, Cyph, she's good to go. Panting almost, man. Her little hummingbird heart's gonna blow."

"If it does, man, then that's a 'que sera sera' type of deal. We've still got mama bear over here."

Angie tried to move her legs and found herself immobile. Her brain was receiving too much stimulus. Her signals were crossed; sounds were registering as scents, scents as colors. Everything swirled together and pulsed rotten around her. She could feel branches scratching against window panes, old souls tired from the weather, wanting a good sleep, the smell of her dead mother's sweat on the couch beneath her, the sick smell of Cypher's breath, the sharp odor of her daughter's fear. Too much again, like that night in the woods. Angie would be a witness to her own undoing, two hyper-sensitive eyes taking in the last moments of her life and Kaya's. It felt like her fate was winding up at fever pitch, anxious to move on to the next soul.

Motion from too many directions and she felt things going wrong so quick, and so surely. She knew Cypher was sliding her sweatpants off and that he had set the gun down when he recognized how gone she was. When Cypher dropped her pants, there was a dull pinging sound—perhaps the fork falling from her pants pocket, she thought—but he paid it no notice. His full attention was on her.

She tried to move again, tried to lift her arm to smack Cypher away from her so she could get to her daughter, but her attempts at motion turned into twitches, light muscle-spasms. Her flesh was deep in mutiny, immobile and begging for death.

Everything was allowed into her head at once, the sound of crickets in the woods beyond her house, the rasp of her underwear sliding off her thighs, the low thrum of the voice inside her head, not even speaking words anymore, just a low, deep note that vibrated through her skin and pulled her heart closer to the ground like gravity amplified by sound. Angie heard whispers, *that's a good girl, just like mama,* and looked over to see Kaya sucking on one of O'Rourke's index fingers, and she knew that her daughter was being tested, that O'Rourke was scared of biters, and that her daughter was going to know too much, too late, and she turned to scream, to turn her voice into a mallet that would crush O'Rourke's skull and splinter it to pieces, but found that her vocal cords were as numb to her as her legs. Kaya must have caught the motion of Angie's head though, because their eyes made contact for a moment, and then Kaya's eyes reflected fear and she was looking down at where Cypher had ignited a long butane utility lighter.

The flame shot out of the end, coming to a sharp point that swallowed the air around it. Cypher had the lighter turned on full; Angie could hear the gas whipping through the long tube to the point where it became a blazing spike. The sound became a taste, boiling blood on her tongue, the sensation turning carbon black, converting to a cry that her lips couldn't form.

Cypher had become silent, intent. He drew the flame lightly and quickly across the surface of her body. She could feel her skin tighten against the heat, but he never kept it in one place long enough to really burn. He brought the flame close to her face. She shrieked inside as the heat came across her open eyes. The flame was close enough that her eyelashes curled back toward their lids, singed black.

She could imagine the moment when Cypher would press the fire into her skin. Would he burn her face first or did he want to watch the pain in her expressions? Would he ignite her hands, each finger a blackening candle? Would he open her up between her legs and re-ignite the long metal snout inside her like a sick mechanical butterfly rooting deep in a flower? She pictured the flame, burning through her from inside....

Her panicked thought was thrown from her mind when she felt the flame settle home on the inside of her left thigh. Cypher left it there for only a moment, long enough to blister the surface of the skin.

The feeling came to her as searing white-hot pain and waves of sound, freight-train insect laughter that sped her pulse until she felt she would pass out. She struggled against unconsciousness and shock.

If I black out, this ends. If I black out, Kaya ends too. Fight.

Cypher moved the flame close to her thigh again. Watching his steady hand and slightly smiling face, she knew she would be burned slowly. That Cypher would help her to understand what it is to burn, to feel skin blacken, boil, and turn to ash. Her pants were off for a reason. Cypher was going to give her an *exact* understanding. He had not forgotten what she had done, and would exact Old-Testament-angry-God-revenge. Slowly. He would keep her alive until her body quit fighting.

Angie inhaled the thin smoke of her skin, a sick smell that filled her senses. The room was heavy with it even though her burn was barely the size of a quarter. She saw smoke floating to the ceiling, pooling in tiny wisps that swam over each other.

I can't take much more. It's not right. I shouldn't....

She turned her head away as much as she could, unable to stop anything, and saw O'Rourke trying to force Kaya's jaw open again, to push his slicked finger back into her warm mouth. She shrieked, staring at her mother wide-eyed again, clearly not believing that a man could be slowly incinerating a woman in front of her.

O'Rourke seized upon the scream and slid his finger back into her mouth. Angie saw the look in Kaya's eyes. She'd become feral. She bit down hard, tiny jaw muscles clenching, and Angie saw the blood from O'Rourke's finger trickling from the corner of Kaya's mouth. He tried to pull his hand away, but only succeeded in stripping skin from bone. He balled his other hand into a fist and swung at the side of Kaya's head.

Kaya thumped back onto the couch, cutting through a thin layer of smoke as she hit the cushions.

Then O'Rourke was upon her. His hands were around Kaya's throat. He was raising her up in the air, squeezing as hard as he could.

To the left Angie could see Cypher's face illuminated by the flame from the utility lighter, smiling behind a tiny plume of black smoke rising from her right inner thigh. He was letting the pointed flame bore in now, melting away skin and fat and muscle, waiting to blacken bone and boil marrow. The pain was so great that her senses sent it through her whole body, an agony-vibration that wrapped razor-wire tight around her heart and sent her pulse interstellar.

To her right, she was watching her daughter die, a man's hands tight around the girl's throat. The pain, the shock of it, seemed muted by comparison.

The vision was here. It was real and she had returned to save her daughter. Or maybe she had just returned to bear witness. An allowance by the thing from the woods, one final grace note to ensure Angie's destruction.

I can't fight this. I can't fight this anymore.

STOP ALL STOP NOW QUIET UNDER QUIET UNDER QUIET.

Angie let go. She stared into her daughter's eyes as they began to bulge from her head. It didn't make sense. Nothing made sense. This world was not for her. She let go and watched.

The voices were right all along.

She tried to communicate with her eyes. She tried as a last effort to comfort Kaya by keeping her sight on her. She let her eyes say, "Let go. Just let go and sleep."

Kaya looked back with hatred.

Her eyes looked directly into Angie's despite the large hands that were wrapped around Kaya's throat. Angie realized that this was the last thing she would ever see.

Angie could not accept *this* fate. She tried to move, tried to yell to her daughter, but could not make a sound.

Angie's eyes filled with fresh anger, a fire in them begging to be let loose, to scorch this atrocity from the face of the earth.

She would not watch her daughter die. She had to do something or she'd face an eternity staring into her daughter's hate-filled eyes. There was no greater hell.

Still she burned in silence, listening to the soft rasp of Cypher's laughter, and noted that he now had his free hand wrapped around his flaccid cock, stroking it as if his revenge could somehow feed it or give him back what he'd lost.

Angie saw motion behind O'Rourke; her eyes picked up a flash of steel that left silver tracers across her field of vision. Whatever or whoever was moving in the dark behind O'Rourke was waiting for an opening. A distraction.

Angie forced her lips to part. She inhaled and then released her anger the only way she knew how. Her scream tore through the room, high-pitched, ragged, the shriek of an animal moments from death.

Cypher and O'Rourke turned to Angie at the same time, unable to ignore the wounded bellow that she forced from her chest with the last of her strength.

Angie saw motion again from the dark. Silver tracers arcing down, exploding in a spray of dark red. Angie couldn't make sense of the sight. Her pupils were blasted, taking on too much information. She was saturated in color, the echo of her scream.

She forced her eyes to focus and saw that O'Rourke was on the floor. Curtis Loew was on top of him, pressing down on the hilt of the survival knife that he'd buried in O'Rourke's belly just beneath his rib cage. Angie could see a bit of gleaming white skull peaking out from the back of Curtis' head, but somehow he was still moving, pushing down on the knife, grunting, growling. O'Rourke's hands were flopping across the shag carpet like asphyxiating fish.

Kaya was looking straight at Angie. The hate had drained from her eyes, replaced by something stranger. Through her crushed throat she managed to say, "Mom."

Then Angie was fighting, trying to pull away from Cypher who was on his knees and had her left leg pinned with his right arm. She struggled, but could barely find the strength to move. She saw Cypher reaching back for his pistol, ready to re-assert control over this unexpectedly fucked scenario.

The sound was small, barely there at all. Still Angie heard it from her right ear, a terrible small screeching noise that struggled to be heard. The fury in it, though, brought goosebumps to Angie's skin.

The high-pitched noise was emerging from Kaya's crushed windpipe as she charged at Cypher with Rusky's old fork in her hand.

Curtis saw it. Angie saw it. It couldn't have been real and yet they both saw the attack. Kaya, their delicate angel, had become something darker, an old harpy hungry to tear flesh from bone as if it was all she understood.

Cypher never reached his gun. The fork went into his throat once, then again. Kaya wasn't stabbing, she was *digging*. She bent the fork as it went in and pulled out as hard as she could. Cypher's throat opened up wide, covering Kaya in arterial spray with every pulse of his heart. She stabbed his throat again, tearing at his larynx so that his cries became a gargled gasp from the hole in his throat. Then she went for his belly, stabbing over and over, tearing skin loose in thin shreds.

Cypher never even fought back. He never had a chance to raise one hand in defense. The look in his eyes as he flopped to the floor said, "This can't be real."

The look was mirrored in the eyes of everyone in the room.

They had reached their understanding.

Kaya turned and looked back at her mother and over her right shoulder at Curtis, who had slid off of O'Rourke's corpse and appeared to be unconscious again.

Kaya was soaked in blood and shaking. She dropped the fork

to the floor.

She tried to shout to her mother, but only managed a whisper. "Can you hear them, Mom? Can you hear them?"

Then she stood, turned toward the front door, and ran off into the dark in her bloody nightshirt. An after-image remained in Angie's iris, a thin, light thousand-fold trace of her daughter.

Angie's legs were a mess, pocked by muscle-deep burn marks. The black and yellow blisters that surrounded the burns looked as if they were moving, boiling.

She tried to stand, but her knees buckled beneath her. She tried again, squeezing her naked thighs tight despite the pain that shot through her burns. She cried out at the feeling, a raw noise that sounded as if it were torn from her throat before it could become a sound.

Still she kept her feet under her and ran out the front door. Angie rounded the corner of the house in time to see a white shape about Kaya's height running into the woods behind Colleen's house. Angie crossed the back yard, her bare feet tearing up old dry leaves and weeds as she ran.

Angie knew that the woods skewed north and were bordered on the west by more suburbs, on the east by farmland. She knew Kaya would stick to the woods, and the agricultural area that bordered it. *She could feel it.*

Entering the forest, Angie frantically swung her head from side to side, searching as her eyes adjusted to the dark of the woods. The canopy had cut off much of her moonlight and a mist was rising from the forest floor. Angie moved toward the barbed-wired border on the eastern side where the light was better and followed the fence line.

She listened for footfalls and heard none. Kaya was smaller than she was and much faster. There had been such terror in her eyes, such disbelief. She was running fast, burning on an engine stoked by fear without end, without comfort.

Time compressed as she stumbled along.

Is this taking hours or minutes? she wondered, then had her answer as she saw the sun coming up, rimming the hills to the east with a sickly yellow glow.

Angie felt a presence to her right and she turned. She saw a cow pond with an old fence post rising from its center. A corpse of dead leaves and old sticks hung on the post. A corpse hung on the post. It smiled at her with its leaves. It spoke without moving it's brittle, wooden jaw.

FALLEN FOR A MOMENTS FIGHT NOTHING.

Angie ignored the voice and turned away, but shivered at its confidence.

If it's fate, then it's going to happen anyway. Why listen to it if I can't escape it?

BRING HER BRING HER LAST LINE BURNT DOWN NOW.

Her? Kaya? You can't have her.

SHE YOU ARE US ALREADY QUIET SOON NOW QUIET.

"No!" Angie ran on, burning inside as her traumatized leg muscles fought to keep her upright and moving.

I can't lose her. Not after all this. If I was her, where would I be headed? We're blood if nothing else. If her fate is mine, then she must be like me. So where would I go?

Angie stopped and breathed heavy at the answer.

I'd go deeper into the woods. I'd get as far away as possible from what happened in the house.

And if the voices are in her now, that's exactly where they'd want her. Far away from anyone else. Alone.

Angie turned away from the fence and the open fields, and moved as quickly as she could through the forest. She turned where she felt she should and hoped Kaya had felt the same way. There were times when she thought she was lost, completely lost, that Kaya had headed in any other direction than the one Angie had taken, and she could barely command her legs to keep moving. She felt serum running down her legs as her blisters burst.

As the sun began to fill the forest, Angie had nearly lost hope. The light shone too bright into her acid-scorched eyes. She could find nothing, no evidence of Kaya's passing, no footprints on the forest floor.

LOST JUST SLEEP SHE IS WITH US NOW JOIN HER.

The voice kept Angie going. If Kaya really was dead, she thought, then why would the voice bother to say it. If it was true, then Angie was as good as dead too and the voice knew it. It knew everything that passed through her mind. Why would it bother to pound away at her if her fate was sealed?

The sunlight that was creeping into the sky was dangerous. The more Angie could see of the forest, the less she wanted to.

She felt as if the forest floor could open up at any minute and swallow her. She felt the floor of the forest sucking at the bottoms of her bare feet. The earth itself was pulling her in, ready to fill her lungs with dirt and leave a bit of her hair blowing in the wind across the forest floor.

To her left, a pile of dead wood surrounded by rhododendrons was twisting, creaking, whispering to her.

Fighting for nothing. So tired, child. So tired.

"Quiet!" Her voice echoed in the woods, but nothing stirred.

She yelled for Kaya as loud as she could. Nothing. Then the voice, crashing through her head.

YOU WILL FALL AND NEVER RISE.

Sunlight, a bright burst in her eye, and she was on the forest floor on her knees with one hand pressed against crackling leaves and her belly was emptying itself out on the ground. Her heart was beating and intact, but her insides felt like they were trying to leave her body. Angie's vomit was pouring out in a constant stream, a sick gush of bile and acid that foamed on the soil.

It's trying to kill me. It's trying to make me listen. It's never done this before.

As she stood and ran, she could feel drops of her blood ooze down her legs from newly formed cracks in her crisped flesh.

She felt surrounded and alone, *so* alone.

Then she heard Kaya's voice a few feet to her left. The sound came from a small clearing, and Angie ran to it.

"You can sleep now, please sleep." It was Kaya's voice.

But she can't know I'm here. Who is she speaking to?

Oh, Jesus. She's talking to herself.

The voice is inside her too.

Angie knew it was true even before she saw her daughter lying on the ground, mouthing words silently to herself.

Kaya's breast gently rising and falling told Angie that her daughter was still alive. But it didn't make sense because the child's chest was half-hollow. The left side of her rib-cage, the side facing up toward the sun, had become wooden and cracked. The wind whipped through it freely, carrying with it the scent of Kaya's last meal, pasta and red sauce. Kaya's right side, however was still flesh, and housed a visible lung and parts of organs that looked loosely organized, slipped from their structure. Hundreds of tiny white flowers were blooming where her heart should have been.

A root had sprung from Kaya's left leg. Thick, wooden, and knotted, it dug deep into the soil. *Like the roots that grew from the rose on my arm.* Angie knew the root functioned in reverse, that it was pulling life from Kaya.

She fell to the ground and reached down to the root, to pull it from the earth, to stop whatever was below from feeding on her daughter, from sucking her dry.

The root was warm, too warm, and Angie felt a faint pulse through the thin bark. It wouldn't budge from the soil. Angie pictured its tendrils twisting hundreds of feet into the ground, feeding something that squirmed in the dark and stared blind through a thousand pale eyes.

Angie tried to bite the root, to sever the tie, but felt only the tips of her teeth splitting, stripping bark and pushing splinters into her gums.

Her mouth was full of old things, her own blood, soil that had seen centuries.

JOIN HER JOIN HER JOIN HER JOIN HER QUIET LIE DOWN.

She turned to Kaya's face. The orbit around her child's right eye had begun to protrude and harden, the eye itself appearing as a twisted knot. The left eye was open and stared dead ahead.

Angie looked into it and tried to find her daughter. "Mama's here, Kaya. I'm here. Please don't let this thing take you, don't let it have you, don't give in. Not now. I've come so far to be with you. I didn't give up."

Angie tried to brush the light hair away from the human side of her face, but tiny white roots began to cover Kaya's skin wher-ever Angie touched. The tips of the roots oozed a thin black fluid that rolled down her daughter's face, over her eyes like obsidian tears.

"They can't have you, Kaya. They can't. You have a reason to be here. You're a good person."

Angie crawled around Kaya, and tried to curl her body up against the shape that was slowly becoming less and less of her child. She let her left arm drape across the sticks that formed Kaya's chest. Thin ribbons of vine crawled up between them and knit Angie's arm to her daughter's ribcage. Angie felt a pain inside her chest and right arm and knew that a rose was blooming beneath her skin. She didn't care.

All she wanted was to pull Kaya away from the earth and carry her home.

All she felt was her own body sinking into the forest floor.

She whispered and she pleaded even when she felt her own jaw stiffen and realized that she could no longer move if she wanted to.

She saw the delicate white flowers that had formed Kaya's heart begin to wilt and blow away, scattered among the old brown leaves.

"No, Angel, please please stay. Please stay. Don't listen to the voice. Don't believe it. It's killing us. It wants to swallow us. There's no peace there. Please come back. I swear, I'll be a good mother to you. I'll never go away again. I'll never go away, and I'll hold you and keep you safe. I'll change. We can dance together. We can have a good life."

Angie felt the forest shaking beneath her and heard her daughter's body creaking as it rubbed up against her. There were no sounds of skin on skin. They were being eaten alive and no bones would be found. They would leave only a tangle of wood that animals would somehow know to avoid.

"I'll be good, Kaya. This whole family is wrong. It has been forever, but we can be different, maybe, if we have each other. If we're not alone."

The forest shook again. Angie heard branches breaking and falling to the ground behind her. Then the voice was upon her, emptied of its shallow promises and full of anger.

NOTHING NOTHING NOTHING YOU WORTHLESS BITCH NOTHING YOU DESERVE NOTHING JUST DIE JUST FALL AND FAIL IT'S ALL YOU'VE EVER DONE AND NO ONE CAN EVER LOVE YOU WOULD EVER LOVE YOU

It's scared. It's lying. Curtis loves me. He said as much.

He's probably dead right now. And for what? To save Kaya and me. A man isn't willing to die defending something worthless.

It's scared.

Angie persisted, doing the only thing she could. She whispered into Kaya's ear and had to hope that her voice was louder than the one that was trying to control their minds.

"Kaya, baby, I love you so much. I've always loved you. I've just been weak. I've been small."

SHUT UP SHUT UP SHE'S GONE UNDER YOU'RE WITH HER ALWAYS IN HER WE CAN TASTE YOU SO SAD SO ALONE YOU WANTED DEATH YOU WANTED HER DEAD.

It's lying.

The only thing I want now is for us to live.

Clouds swallowed up the sunshine above and the clearing became cold. The warm smell of decay that floated up from Kaya did not go away despite the chill.

"I'm with you Kaya. I'm with you. I'm with...."

Angie found her tongue was no longer her own. It had become solid, immovable. Vines crept up the back of her neck and wrapped around her forehead. She saw her right arm had blossomed, but the leaves of the rose had already given in to rot and were dropping to her ruptured skin below.

Angie fought against her bindings. She managed to free her left arm, and plunged her left hand into the area where Kaya's heart

should have been. Little white petals scattered from her trespass. She held her hand strong despite new roots that reached from the ground and tried to twist her arm back.

There, at the center of her hand, she felt the beating of her daughter's heart. There was a heat to it, a burning light that felt as old as the darkness that was swallowing them both. She clenched her hand into a fist and held it tight, although it felt like her hand was now on fire.

She brought the hand to her mouth and it warmed her tongue. She could feel its fibers relaxing, become muscle again, soft and wet. She whispered her love into her white-knuckled fist, then opened her hand and breathed in her daughter's heartbeat.

The fire was through her in seconds, the rose that sprouted from her arm became a burning spire that blew to ash.

She could hear her daughter's heartbeat running counter to her own, flushing through her body, making her warm, making her whole again. The voice beneath the constant rapid thump of Kaya's heart sounded so distant.

you will never be never heal never whole and always alone

And the pounding became so loud and strong that it was all Angie could hear. Her body shook. She sat up, feeling a strength she'd never known. She reached down to free Kaya's leg from the ground. The rooted limb would not pull free. The root blackened at her touch and began to burn, but too quickly, and soon all of Kaya's body was aflame, crackling, spewing smoke.

Angie let her burn. She knew where her daughter was. She could feel Kaya in her blood.

She watched the shape that had been her daughter smolder and crumble until it was a pile of ash in the shape of a girl. The clouds above began to sprinkle rain and the forest smelled clean and moist.

Angie sat cross-legged beside Kaya's funeral pyre and began to eat her ashes.

The new whispers in her blood had taught her this.

The same whispers consoled her and caressed her inside as her belly filled tight and her throat was coated in ash.

Angie let the cold rain soak her skin. Her daughter's heartbeat, pounding loud and fast inside her head, rocked her into a peaceful state.

There was no pain or blood during the birth. Angie felt only life as she opened her legs to the rain, a warm and true sense of life that had long escaped her. Her legs shook and she felt her pelvis shatter, but there was no pain.

Even after Kaya was born, even after Angie watched her daughter grow from infant to young woman in her arms, she could still hear the distant drum of the heart she'd swallowed.

Angie held her daughter tight in the calm of the woods. Kaya held Angie just as tight.

The rain fell soft on their naked skin as they slept calm in each other's arms.

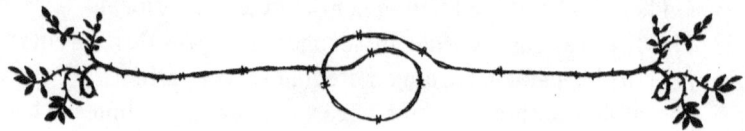

12—With the Current

The headaches bothered Curtis less and less. He figured it was the ocean air. He'd always heard it was good for healing.

He thought the ache in his heart could benefit from a little salt air too. There wasn't a day that passed when he didn't miss Kaya and Angie. He was happy knowing they were okay, happy knowing that he had helped them as much as he could, but the ache didn't fade.

He was without a family again. Sure he got the occasional e-mail from Kaya, but it wasn't the same as spending real time with another human being.

Curtis had known he was losing them. The last time he'd seen them on that terrible day, they'd already seemed dead in a way. Their eyes had held such terror and something else, something darker.

Miss Martinez had found Curtis slumped on top of Patrick O'Rourke's body. She'd come by to check out Kaya's new room, and saw the blood stain on Curtis' floor. She checked out Colleen's house on instinct.

Curtis was comatose for three weeks and had a plate screwed into his skull where it'd been fractured. The post-surgery headaches made his old back pain seem petty by comparison.

No charges were brought against him. He told the story of that day as he knew it. The cops checked out Curtis' story and pegged it as true after seeing Cypher and O'Rourke's rap sheets. A kidnapping warrant was issued for Angie. She'd never had legal custody. The cops couldn't locate her or Kaya.

When the two Smith women showed up at the Palm Center Physical Therapy Clinic asking for his help and offering hugs, the surprise and emotion overwhelmed him. So happy they were alive, he'd begun to cry, but he pushed the emotions down to keep from upsetting them.

He'd helped them over the next couple of weeks although the nature of their request made him cry on his bad headache days. All they wanted from him was two fake IDs, two fake passports, one fake history.

Curtis was not part of their plan.

He found someone online who he could pay to do the job in a rush. The ID's were questionable, but their new history seemed rock solid. He'd planted a brand new family tree for them.

He'd asked Angie why one night, why they didn't want him to go with them.

"Something changed that day, Curtis. I'm so thankful for what you did for us and I need you to understand that. You saved our lives. You showed me something about myself. But for a while... I'm sorry, I can't explain this better... but for a while, Kaya and I only need each other. But I promise we'll stay in contact."

And they did. They e-mailed when they could and they seemed like they were doing okay.

After buying his RV with the last of his payout from the paper mill, Curtis met new people. No one he'd like to start a family with, but nice people none the less. They liked him. Strangers treated him to meals in different states and taught him how to play cribbage.

This week he'd driven all the way to San Diego. He loved the warm breeze that swept in off the beach and the strength of the waves.

He sat at the window of his RV for a while, looking out, watching the scattered crowds of beach goers enjoying the balmy off-season. Finally he tired of watching from a distance and walked barefoot down to the surf. The ocean was so big, so wide and strong and constant.

He was afraid for a moment, feeling the water's strong pull on his ankles as the waves swept back out to sea.

He thought of Kaya and Angie, alone somewhere in the world, creating new lives out of nothing. He'd tried to warn them, but didn't know exactly what to warn against. He'd said to Angie, "It's such a huge world. There's so much trouble, so much violence. Things are just too ugly. The murders…there are more of them everyday, these murders that don't make sense. I never want you and Kaya to be hurt, not ever again."

Angie had been straight with her response. "Curtis, I'm kind of depending on things being fucked up out there. It'll be easier for us to hide. The cops have got their hands full without worrying about us. Besides, I can't imagine Kaya or me ever being worse off than we already were. Even if something happened to me, she's strong. She's a survivor."

Curtis couldn't help the vision that popped into his head. A little girl swinging a bloody fork over and over again.

Christ. They've already handled the roughest cards they could be dealt.

"You're right, Angie. Still, if you ever need me…."

Those had been his last words to Angie. It had been harder to watch Kaya go.

He thought of his last moment with Kaya, of their final embrace, a goodbye hug that cracked his heart wide open and had him fighting tears. He had stayed strong for Kaya, not crying, trying to make it easy for her to go. Always the stone man.

When she said, "Thank you, Curtis," he began to shake. She was acknowledging the bizarre truth that even Curtis was having difficulty wrapping his injured mind around.

I saved their lives.

He'd been surprised when she whispered, "I love you, Curtis," followed by "Goodbye." His tears came later, his pain offset by a new pride.

Now the ocean water was pulling at his ankles. He stepped in deeper and let it carry him out.

Soon the sea was holding him and he floated, arms and legs wide, listening to the waves crash against the shore. He heard people laughing on the beach, enjoying their time together.

He began laughing, too. The headache that had been creeping into his day subsided as if it had been washed away.

That night he met a soft-spoken woman named Patricia who joined him for some barbecued chicken. She said he smelled like the ocean.

When he kissed her, he tasted sea salt on her lips.

In his whole life, nothing had ever tasted better.

13—Phoenix

The two women were marked by scars.

The young one had a wrist that ached on rainy days and she often had difficulty grasping heavy objects with her left hand.

The older one had a thick scar on her left cheekbone and knotted burn scars on her legs.

Anyone could see these things.

Anyone watching us, thought Angie, *would know that we're running. What they wouldn't know is that the farther we run away from our past, the closer we're coming to something else. Something better.*

She had her moments of doubt. Things weren't always easy with Kaya, and Angie worried about how much the young woman might be just like her mom. But she held out hope.

Kaya talked to her. Constantly. A dam had broken after that day in the woods. Years of childhood questions had been stored. Not all of them were pretty.

"Why did you leave me with Colleen?" Kaya had asked.

It was a question that made Angie feel weak and small. It made her feel like reaching for a bottle, some pills, a gun. She felt like running.

But she didn't, not this time. She had answers. Some were ugly. Many made no sense to her although her actions had felt right at the time.

Things feel so true when they're happening. Voices sound so real, blinding lights seem dimmer with time.

163

The voice from the woods never came back into Angie's head, or Kaya's. Angie felt she and Kaya had destroyed it, whatever it was, although there were times she questioned *its* existence at all.

But if it wasn't real?

Angie refused the idea. If the voice had been created by her own mind, the threat was absolute and inescapable. She couldn't face that.

Angie wondered about the crooked family tree Curtis had unearthed. Was her entire family really cursed? The voice had whispered of corrupted blood lines.

If it was in my blood, in Kaya's blood, then it's been burned clean. Curses break, old things die squealing. If we were haunted, if we were sick from birth, we've done our detox.

She'd felt her past, the thick possibilities of her ancestor's wrongs, on her body like a parasite, pulling the life from her. Kaya had helped her to break free, to loosen the purchase of old, embedded teeth.

Something wonderful had delivered her from her waking nightmare. She refused to pin it all on madness or bad blood.

No. Whatever happened, no matter how wrong it was, no matter how surreal... it happened. I felt it. I heard it. I knew these things.

I was there. So was Kaya. The way she looks at me now, and the way my heart beats....

Angie wondered what would ever happen should they separate. In the moments she thought of leaving Kaya, she could still feel *something* that had ebbed begin to flow through her mind. Something old, and strong that wanted into her head.

Sometimes old things just need to rest.

Whispers could be subtle. Angie never let Kaya get too far from her sight.

As they traveled from state to state, Angie found she still had trouble connecting with people. It had been a long time since she'd trusted herself, let alone another human being.

She tried to follow Kaya's cue. When Kaya smiled at a waitress, Angie tried to offer up the same. She trusted her daughter's instincts.

Kaya was the one who let Curtis close. If she hadn't trusted someone, we'd both be dead.

Angie thought of Curtis. Perhaps, in a couple of years, she'd invite him to come out to Phoenix.

Something about Phoenix appealed to them. Whatever it was, the heat, the open space of the desert, it made them consider settling down for the first time in months. Traveling took its toll and they were starting to get on each other's nerves.

At first they had carried a strange euphoria with them. The feeling, this strange warmth, stayed with them for weeks after their time in the woods.

The physical feeling faded with time, but their new connection remained. They'd always been blood, but there was something more now.

Neither of them mentioned the strange dreams they'd been having. The visions of barbed wire, broken wood, blazing fire, and rain.

Neither of them mentioned the strange sensation in their chests. It was like having two heartbeats. A rapid pulse would beat separate from their own when the other was upset. It was disorienting, so they seldom fought.

And when they held each other at night, they could feel the pulse unify, one great and steady heart, beating ocean-strong. The sound of blood moving carried with it the greatest promise, although the two women never spoke directly of it after waking.

The promise:
That they had each other
and
That they were alive.

The Intersection of Amiable Madmen—
An Authors' Note

The creation of *Siren Promised* began at the tail-end of 2002, born from the authors' shared concepts about certain elements of the human experience and their desire to collaborate on another project after the mind-blowing, med-shock meltdown that was *Pain and Other Petty Plots to Keep You in Stitches*.

As a collaborative experience, *Siren Promised* came to life via a series of brainstorming and editing sessions that included the review of hundreds of Alan's paintings. Alan and Jeremy decided that the artwork chosen and developed for the story should do more than just illustrate. There would be as little description of the images in the story as possible. Why create duplication? The subject matter for each piece would be based on the characters' subjective experiences instead of being limited to depictions of actions and environments specifically embodied in the text. Each image would arise from a character's memory, visualization, fantasy or hallucination. In this way the artwork that was chosen before writing began would inform the writers about each character's perspective. An odd approach to be sure, but a fascinating process of discovery.

Approximately thirty paintings were chosen as springboards for the story, and as Jeremy and Alan engaged in a marathon discussion, a plot outline emerged. Concepts for new paintings were then proposed and the writing began.

Alan entrenched himself with Curtis Loew while Jeremy spent too much time in the mind of Angie Smith. Despite the two-author/two-character/one-story structure, the work went smoothly. The characters quickly took on lives of their own and became equal partners in the writing process.

An example from a phone conversation:

"Hey, Jeremy?"

"Yeah, Alan."

"Curtis killed Colleen today, sort of. Is that going to be a problem?"

"Sweet mother of Christ, Clark. We had three chapters planned with her."

"Yeah, well... too late."

The culmination of this collaborative process was the strange dark book you're holding now. If you've read *Siren Promised*, thank you. We hope you've enjoyed reading it as much as we enjoyed creating it. If you're just skipping ahead, knock it off, go back to page one, and buckle up.

—Alan M. Clark & Jeremy Robert Johnson
Oregon, U.S.A.
May 2004

The Artwork

Although the pieces of artwork appearing in this volume were often revised to better suit their use in *Siren Promised*, they are listed here by their original titles.

In order of appearance:

"Siren Promised" (cover art) original to this volume

"The Mind Wanders" originally appeared on the cover of *Things Left Behind* - Gary A. Braunbeck - Cemetery Dance Publications

"Penetration" originally appeared with "Penetration" - Joseph Citro - Thunder's Shadow Magazine

"Study #2 for 'The Sticks'" originally appeared in *A Haunting in Tennessee, the Bell Family Spirit* - Scorpius Digital Publishing

"The Rose" originally appeared in *Exit at Toledo Blade Boulevard* - Jack Ketchum - Obsidian Press

"Entrada" originally appeared with "Entrada" - Mary Rosenblum - Asimov's Science Fiction

"Vapors" originally appeared with "Vapors" - Jack Dann - Amazing Stories

"Deadfall" Originally appeared as cover art for Iniquities Magazine

"Her Hunger" Originally appeared in *Night Visions 10* edited by Richard Chizmar - Subterranean Press

"Twins" originally appeared in *The Graves* - Alan M. Clark - Gauntlet Publications

"For You, the Living" originally appeared on the cover of *For You, the Living* - Wayne Allen Sallee - Roadkill Press

"To Know Them By Heart" originally appeared in *Darkside: Horror for the Next Millennium* edited by John Pelan - Darkside Press

"The Beggar in the Living Room" originally appeared with "The Beggar in the Living Room" - William John Watkins - Asimov's Science Fiction

"Garbage at Dawn" originally appeared in *Imagination Fully Dilated* edited by Elizabeth Engstrom & Alan M. Clark - Cemetery Dance Publications

"Stoneman" originally appeared with "Stone Man" - Wennicke Eide - Asimov's Science Fiction

"The One on the Roof" originally appeared in *Imagination Fully Dilated* edited by Elizabeth Engstrom & Alan M. Clark - Cemetery Dance Publications

"Flirting with Death" original to this volume

"Green Fire" original to this volume

"River Stones Cannot See" originally appeared in *Not Broken, Not Belonging* - Randy Fox - Roadkill Press

"Nuclear Shadows" originally appeared in *Imagination Fully Dilated, Volume II* edited by Elizabeth Engstrom - IFD Publishing

"Came to Rest" originally appeared in *Not Broken, Not Belonging* - Randy Fox - Roadkill Press

"A Branch in the Wind" originally appeared in *Flaming Arrows* - Bruce Holland Rogers - IFD Publishing

"Shambling Things" original to this volume

"No Chance to Think" original to this volume

"Delicate Angel" original to this volume

"Half Scairt" originally appeared in *Not Broken, Not Belonging* - Randy Fox - Roadkill Press

"Rhododendron Hell" originally appeared in *Not Broken, Not Belonging* - Randy Fox - Roadkill Press

"No Bones Will Be Found" original to this volume

"Barbed Wire Rose" original to this volume

"Hearth Stone" original to this volume

"Vinegar Woods" originally appeared on the cover of *Midnight Promises* - Richard Chizmar - Gauntlet Publications

Duct Tape Is Not a Food: An After-Afterword

by Jeremy Robert Johnson

Clark and I managed to pack a lot of nasty business into a pretty short novel. And honestly, I'm proud we managed to get away with it—to be able to pull the audience into a world of drugs and rape and murder and paranoia and loneliness and make them want to keep reading—that takes a lot of work.

Sympathy doesn't come easy for anybody. If you felt something for, or experienced something with Curtis and Angie, then Clark and I did our jobs.

But why'd we have to make things so ugly? I wondered that myself sometimes, finger hovering over the delete key, anxious to erase what I felt were naked emotional truths on display.

We had our reasons. The brutality of Siren Promised wasn't wholly gratuitous. Partially? Okay, maybe. But not wholly.

Was the reason to shock? Nope. Shock is easy. The default setting for the lazy writer. Watch—Jesus rapes babies! See—shock is easy. And eventually boring.

Was the reason to edify? In a way. As much as I adore Simon Clark's lovely intro, I do not personally ask that you learn from Siren Promised. You live on Earth. You already know the generalized party line—Drugs Are Bad. You saw the same After School Special where Helen Hunt takes a bunch of acid and eats Scott Baio's face, or whatever. So while Siren Promised could help to cement a particularly antagonistic view of drugs, it's not likely to save America's youth from any chemical scourge (can you imagine them teaching this book to High School kids?).

But what I do hope for is that some reader, some day, might pick up this book and really be able to relate to it. Because we kept things raw, and ugly, and didn't shy away from putting our guts on the page. Because we didn't put on our rose-colored glasses and pretend there was ever anything easy about addiction, even for those who rise above it. And maybe the underlying theme of struggle and redemption, as experienced through the characters, will resonate and give that person a little strength. Maybe the book could

171

even reinforce a person's resolve like Rand's Atlas Shrugged did for me when I was going through a particularly rough time (only our readers won't have to absorb all that capitalist propaganda).

So, there's my pipe-dream. Hokey? Maybe. But cynicism is for lazy people.

The other reason this book gets so ugly is, for me, a selfish one, and has much to do with Simon Clark's line about "personal weaponry." Siren Promised, and some of my first fiction collection Angel Dust Apocalypse, act as reminders. Permanent Post-It notes for myself saying, "This is what will happen when you start chasing your rock-bottom again." So far, it seems to be working. I've even had a painting from this book ("No Bones Will Be Found") tattooed as a sleeve around my right forearm. Talk about reminders.

Thanks, by the way, for watching me work out my own weird shit through fiction. From a lot of the wonderful responses I've received, I'm guessing many of you are going through very similar brands of weird shit too. It's been great having you share your amusing and occasionally frightening stories with me. Especially the guy who tried to eat a roll of duct tape when he was high on mescaline. Up until then I'd always thought I was the only one that'd ever happened to. It gets so hard to keep chewing, doesn't it?

Also, for those who have asked, I'm not anti-drug myself, but anti-abuse and pro-education. It's sad that humans are just generally so terrible at utilizing drugs. It puts a huge damper on potentially beneficial uses like pain reduction, neural re-growth, religious worship, therapy, etc.

And to the readers who didn't quite grasp the crux of my drug-related fiction—Please do not offer to send me drugs, or give me drugs in person (no, not even at Burning Man, as much as that pains me to say it). Even custom engineered phenyl-whatevers, as fascinating as I find those analogs. I appreciate your kindness and enthusiasm, truly, and wish you'd been around about four years ago. But I'm trying out a different phase of my life now—chasing down new ways to trigger the treasure-trove of chemicals already stewing in my brain. Lucid dreaming, guided meditation, marathon running, Krav Maga. Holding my breath for a really long time. Things like that. So far, it's been a lot of fun, and I'm anxious to see where this path leads....

A final nod in your direction for picking up what is likely to be one of the first books on the new Bizarro imprint Swallowdown Press. Swallowdown is working hard to bring you underground material (which, for now, means my fiction) at mainstream level quality and is being founded out of admiration for people like Jim Munroe, Carlton Mellick III, and Ian MacKaye. Your continued support of the independent press is helping to keep a lot of hardworking artists alive, and as one member of that troupe, you have my gratitude.

Portland, Oregon
March 2006

About the Authors

Jeremy Robert Johnson is the author of the critically acclaimed cult novel *Skullcrack City*. His fiction has been praised by the *Washington Post*, *Publishers Weekly*, and authors Chuck Palahniuk and David Wong and has appeared internationally in numerous anthologies and magazines. Johnson lives in Portland, Oregon. www.jeremyrobertjohnson.com

More books by Jeremy Robert Johnson:
Angel Dust Apocalypse
Extinction Journals
We Live Inside You
Skullcrack City
Entropy in Bloom

Alan M. Clark is the author and illustrator of eleven novels, including the Jack the Ripper Victims Series, and the memoir/horror fiction novel, *The Surgeon's Mate: A Dismemoir*. As a visual artist, he has created illustrations for hundreds of books, including works of fiction of various genres, nonfiction, textbooks, young adult fiction, and children's books. Awards for his work include the World Fantasy Award and four Chesley Awards. Alan M. Clark and his wife, Melody, live in Oregon. www.alanmclark.com

More books by Alan M. Clark:
The Blood of Father Time Duology (written in collaboration with Stephen C. Merritt and Lorelei Shannon)
D.D. Murphry, Secret Policeman (written in collaboration with Elizabeth Massie)
Of Thimble and Treat: The Life of a Ripper Victim
A Parliament of Crows
The Door that Faced West
Say Anything but Your Prayers
The Surgeon's Mate: A Dismemoir
A Brutal Chill in August
Apologies to the Cat's Meat Man

Recent paperback titles released by IFD Publishing

Bull's Labyrinth, by Eric Witchey
The Surgeon's Mate: A Dismemoir, by Alan M. Clark
Professor Witchey's Miracle Mood Cure, by Eric Witchey
Baggage Check, by Elizabeth Engstrom
Death is a Star, by Christina Lay
How to Write a Sizzling Sex Scene, by Elizabeth Engstrom

Many more titles are available from IFD Publishing in ebooks and audio books.

IFD Publishing, P.O. Box 40776, Eugene OR 97404, U.S.A.
Ph: (541)461-3272
http://www.ifdpublishing.com
contact@ifdpublishing.com